Julie Hiner

Published by Crystal Lake Publishing—Where Stories Come Alive!

Website: www.crystallakepub.com

Torrid Waters is the pulp and extreme horror imprint of Crystal Lake. For this book, the author has not supplied any trigger warnings.

To all those who respect and fear what lives in the deep…

Midnight Swim

Missy never missed a late-night breaststroke along the shoreline, until the night the ocean ate her up.

At this hour, the scantily clad sunbathers and the next Mr. Mission Beach wannabes were packed tight into tequila infused, sweat-soaked bars, indulging in stiff drink buzzes and one-night stands. Missy hated all of that. She preferred the tranquility of a moonlight swim under the diamond covered midnight sky to the sound of crashing waves.

The cool ocean soothed her soul, calming her right to the core. The saltwater rippled around her muscular, tanned body as she glided through the water, on the other side of the surf. Where it was calm. Where it was quiet. Where it was just her and the open water.

Her front stroke was strong. Years of swimming had sculpted her arms and legs into water treading machines. Her mind was clear. Open. Nothing clouded her thoughts. She breathed in rhythm with her strokes. Arms and breath became one. Perfect vision allowed her to swim goggle free, seeing the depths below with raw clarity.

Mid-stroke, a shadow crossed her path. She jolted, treading water, halting her swim. She scanned the water line. No fins poked. No tails popped. No ripples were made. The water stilled like a sheet of glass.

She submerged her face again, clawing at the black strands of hair clinging to her eyes. Scanning the dark water, nothing stirred. Nothing caught her attention. She shrugged it off. It could have been a glimmer from the full moon. Or maybe it was a loose piece of algae, destined to be adrift and lost forever.

Missy took a deep breath, flipped over onto her back, and spun her arms in a perfect, smooth circle The full moon glowed like a celestial sphere, a guide for the entire earth as it spun on its axis. A plethora of stars dotted the ebony sky, like celebratory sparklers frozen in time. It was her own private fireworks of blazing planets.

Her arms propelled her through the cold, dark water, creating a ripple down her legs. She ogled the bursts of twinkles, looking for Aquarius—the first constellation her father had taught her about, when she was six years old. Finding the landmark of her life, she reveled in the glimmering pattern that took her back to a time when life made sense. When a moonlight walk, hand in hand with Dad, learning about the wonders of the universe, was all that mattered.

She closed her eyes, letting the sounds of the ocean wash through her mind. The dense quiet of the vast land beneath the surface was the most soothing sound on the entire planet. At least to her. Out here, there was nothing but the moon, the stars, the water…and her.

Something brushed against her thigh. She froze, raised her torso, treading water again. Scanning the watery horizon, she chuckled to herself then slid onto her back. Her arms resumed their circular motion. The water rippled around her body, down her legs. Closing her eyes, she sunk into the peaceful motion. Breath, body, and ocean all became one.

There it was again, something slippery against her leg. She turned in a circle, investigating her surroundings. Nothing. No ripple. No splash. The water a still sheet.

She shook her head.

Did she imagine it? She really should stop watching those deep-sea horror movies. It was a weird fetish, to watch bloody massacres in the environment she loved most. She couldn't help it. They were hilarious the way they turned the most peaceful setting in the world into a place painted with blood.

Stop being stupid. Her lips twisted into a frown. Barely over the wake, where the water was still, she wasn't far enough out to be concerned about anything large. Or unknown.

She turned onto her back. Her arms resumed a smooth circle.

Two more strokes in and pain shot through her leg. Her eyes bolted open as she let out a cry. Her arms and legs flailed in a manic tread. Plunging a hand into the water, she ran her palm along her thigh down to her foot. Pain sliced through her shin as her fingers sunk into her flesh.

What the hell?

Water splashed as her hand shot up. She stared at her fingers. Her brain seized. Watery blood drenched the tips, slithering down her knuckles and over her wrist. Pulling her leg to the surface, she cradled her shin with her arm, raising it above the watery blanket.

She swallowed as a prickle trickled down her spine. Three puncture marks in her flesh seeped scarlet. Her back clenched. Her mind whirled.

What could leave a bite mark like this?

There were two things that swam along the wake. Dolphins. They were plentiful and playful, dancing along with surfers. And sharks. They were few. And large. She would have seen the fin darting away. Or felt the wake caused by the massive body. And that bite would have been far worse, covering half her leg, or her entire arm.

Missy rescanned the horizon.

The dark water stretched out around her motionless. The moon glowed, casting shimmers of light along the surface. She faced the shore and proceeded with a mock breaststroke, keeping her head above water and seeking the thing that bit her.

Nausea spun her stomach. Bile crawled up her throat. Dizziness spun her mind and her vision blurred.

She shook her head, telling the panic to fuck off.

It didn't work. Maybe it wasn't hysteria. Everything around her crawled along in a lethargic state. It was like the world was moving in slow motion. The moon glowered down at her. The lapping of the waves was the only sound. Her legs were heavy weights, pulling her down.

Pain shot through her other leg. Her eyelids drooped. She pushed her hand down through the jello-like water, seeking the source of the throbbing ache. Her fingers found more sticky holes, this time having pierced her right leg.

Pulling her arm up through the thick water, her hand ripped through the surface. Scarlet syrup clung to her fingers, saltwater thinning it as it trickled down her arm.

A shiver took over her whole body. The beach seemed impossibly far away, but she half swam, half limped toward the stretch of sand glowing under the moonlight.

Sharp teeth grabbed her toes. She screamed. Her arms flailed in a panic induced pathetic swim, trying to reach the beach. Away from whatever was hunting her down below.

Gulping mouthfuls of salt water, she bobbed and shrieked. "Help!"

Something slit her ankle. A fresh gash stung her leg.

She screamed again. "Someone! Please!"

A shadowed figure walked along the boardwalk, on the other side of the beach.

Her stomach clenched as she forced her voice through her throat. "It's got me! Help!" Her pleas scratched against her throat. The distance between the wake and the beach swallowed up her cries like tiny morsels. The figure continued down the boardwalk, turning out of sight.

No.

Shards of pain shot up both her legs as her vision blurred, causing the shoreline to spin. The houses lining the boardwalk swiveled out of control. She gritted her teeth and willed her arms into motion. Battling the wake, she fought against the weight of her arms, digging into the water, pulling herself up and over the wave. She floated down the other side. Her body bobbed up and down in the constant waves. Concentrating hard, she dug her teeth into her bottom lip, piercing the skin. A copper tang drenched her tongue. She swallowed against the stomach acid gurgling at the back of her throat.

Why did her body feel like a heavy heap of sand?

What the hell had bitten her?

Where was it now?

With every labored stroke, metallic salt water kissed her lips and the sandy shore seemed to move away from her. The moonlight glimmered over the houses beyond, swirling them into dream-like visions.

Another slice of pain, across her arm.

"No…!" Her cries dissolved into the night air.

As she forced another stroke, more blood spurted from the fresh wound.

Dread flushed through her veins as she frantically searched for the source of the bite.

A flash of fluorescence lit up the water. A purple haze of light, glowing beneath the sheer, black surface. Her mind strained, a last attempt to comprehend what strange thing was hunting her.

A putrid stench violated her nose, awakening her senses. Her mind shot back to the time she had discovered a dead sea animal, half decomposed, infested with insects, lying in its unfortunate end, exposed on the shore.

She gagged and searched the water, the fluorescent light had vanished.

Please. I don't want to die.

She spun back toward the shore. Her wounded arm refused to move. Treading water with her one functional arm, her legs kicked in a meek attempt to keep her head above water.

Thickness coated her mind. The houses, the beach, the moon, the stars, melded into a thick, cosmic stream as she blinked hard. She dropped her bloody arm back into the water. Her limbs were heavy weights. She was a boat, anchored in place.

Something bit hard into her leg. She gasped. Her eyes darted over the sky, seeking her life's landmark. Aquarius blinked back at her like a beacon. Memories flooded her mind.

The strength of her father's arm around her shoulders, his face, his hand, and his finger pointing up into the night sky.

Fangs bit into her, hard, sinking deep into her flesh, finding bone. Her ankle crunched. The water pulled her down. Aquarius blinked out. The air sucked out of her lungs. The life drained from her body. She surrendered to the black underwater world.

Washed Ashore

The ocean breeze played with her hair as Bailey whipped along the boardwalk. Weaving through pedestrians, cyclists, and skateboarders, she guided the wheels of her tattered pink roller skates with ease. Her feet had been a size five since she was twelve.

The open ocean stretched out across the beach from Belmont Park. The surf was steady. How long had it been since she went out past the wake? She couldn't remember. She didn't want to.

Clusters of people milled around the shabby storefronts lining the cul-de-sac nestled beside the boardwalk. Sunny San Diego had been her home for her entire life, and she loved it. The thought of leaving had never crossed her mind. Even after the accident.

Some people had encouraged her to find a new place, a fresh start. But something in the pit of her gut told her not to listen to them. She couldn't imagine living anywhere else.

Swinging a hard right, she rolled off the curb with a slight jump and landed on the street. Ventura Place, the one block street, snipped the end of Mission Bay Drive, leading directly to the ocean front. People in jean shorts and flip-flops meandered along the walk, browsing sun dresses, bathing suits, and t-shirts with San Diego decals.

Bailey rolled down to the end of the street and maneuvered left. The wheels clinked onto the sidewalk, over a metal ledge, and through a doorway into Don's Grocery.

Stealing a glance at the front counter, she noticed Don wasn't in. Brad, Don's son, manned the cash register, his tousled, bleached blond hair hiding his eyes.

Brad looked up sleepily. "Hey, Bailey."

"Hey, Brad." She rolled past, over to the candy aisle. Eyeballing her options, she settled on her usual. She picked an array of lollipops—cherry, strawberry, orange… And what was this? Sour berry. Bright blue. She shrugged, then plucked one up, adding it to her collection.

She rolled up to the register, piled the colorful array of hard candy onto the counter, and fished some loose change out of her front jean-shorts pocket. The coins clinked against the counter. She counted them out, put a dime back in her pocket, then slid the pile toward Brad.

"Nice day." Brad's voice sounded thick with lethargy and weed.

"As usual."

"Yeah." Brad's eyes threatened to close.

Bailey grabbed the sour berry lollipop and stuffed the rest into her shoulder bag. "See ya."

"Later."

She rolled out of the store, clacked over the metal bar, then wheeled onto the road. At the end of the cul-de-sac, she turned right, picked up speed, and glided along the boardwalk. The ocean called out to her again. She cleared her thoughts and focused on weaving through the people. Pulling the wrapper off the candy, she stuffed it into her pocket and then popped the bright blue ball into her mouth. Her lips puckered. It *was* sour. But kind of sweet too, with a slight berry tinge. She took a long suck, then let the candy settle against her right cheek, causing it to bulge.

Finding a steady rhythm, she scanned the boardwalk ahead.

People trickled along, the crowd from the storefront thinning. Ahead, a mob huddled together, on the beach, at the edge of the shore.

What the hell? There weren't any special events happening today. Not that she knew of. Bulletins advertising all events at every beach along the twenty-seven-mile coastline were posted at all lifeguard stations. Working five shifts a week at the Pacific Beach station, she would have seen a flyer if something attracting dozens of people was planned.

Pushing off her right leg to give herself a boost, she approached the edge of the boardwalk.

Three lifeguard trucks were parked in the sand, two near the shore, the other closer to her. She scanned the crowd but couldn't see any of her coworkers through the thick blanket of people. A police cruiser pulled up, rolling to a stop next to the lifeguard truck closest to the shore. An officer emerged, middle-aged and portly, and strode across the sand, pushing his way through the pack.

Bailey dropped her bag onto the sand and sat on a staircase. She worked fast to untie her skates and remove them, then sat them beside the concrete wall separating the boardwalk from the beach. Her feet sunk into the sand as she scrambled over to the water to join the crowd.

When she reached them, she heard various cries of despair.

"Oh my God," one woman screeched.

"Who is it?" a deep voice asked.

"What happened to her?" a young voice echoed.

Bailey pushed her way into the gathering, wondering if some poor soul had swum out too far and met their match with the strong surf. Three lifeguard trucks were present, but now that she was on scene, it was imperative to find out if she could help.

Folks were growing rowdy, teetering on the brink of panic. The lone officer she'd seen arrive was in the middle of the mob, waving his hands, yelling for people to please go back to the boardwalk. Craig, a fellow guard at the Pacific Beach station, stood at the front of the group. As she closed in on him, an odor stopped her in her tracks. She gagged against the stink of death and rot, like nothing she'd ever smelled before. Creatures of the sea washed ashore on a regular basis, so she'd seen a lot of death on the beach over her years as a lifeguard. But this… This was unreal. Bailey swallowed hard, popped the lollipop out, then breathed through her mouth.

Craig saw her and waved for her to come closer. His blond curls bounced off his shoulders. His red lifeguard suit clung to his muscles. She finally reached him and caught a glimpse of a body on the beach behind him and the two other lifeguards pushing back against the line of people.

Craig yelled over the voices. "This is nuts. As soon we saw the commotion, we drove over. When we spotted the body, we called the police. The officer just arrived. Said backup is on the way." He turned his attention to the restless people, asking them to please move away. They finally responded, letting him guide them back.

That's when she saw the source of the panic and her body froze. She swallowed sour berry-coated saliva as her jaw clenched and her brain seized. The crab on toast she'd had for breakfast churned in her stomach.

The body of a young woman lay exposed on the beach. Her legs and arms were sprawled out, twisted into contortions that seemed impossible. Long, dark hair tangled into a mess around her head, concealing most of her face. Her fingers were bent in a clutch, as if she had been grabbing at something, clawing her way out of whatever horrific destiny had squeezed the life from her.

The red bikini she wore had been ripped, exposing far too much.

Something pulled at her gaze. She walked closer, inspecting the warped limbs. They appeared muscular but pale, drained of life. Examining the mess of black hair tangled with lengths of slimy algae, she tried to see the woman's face. An eye peered through the mane. A small crab crawled out of the clutter, inching its way down the strands and across the glassy eyeball.

Bailey gulped. Three deep, red holes, glared back at her from one of the pallid arms.

She swallowed against the sour berry-soaked bile rising in her throat. *What made a bite mark like that?*

There were multiple bite marks down both her legs, and one below her shoulder, each composed of three deep red wells.

She'd seen this before—the day of the accident. She was sure of it.

The sound of sirens jarred her from her thoughts. The noise from the crowd whirred around her and shouts from the officer rang through the air. The people had moved back a couple of feet, but the officer and the lifeguards had a weak hold on the situation.

"Bailey," Craig yelled.

She sprinted away from the body and over to him.

"Can you run to my truck, the one by the boardwalk, and call the PB station? Ask them to send whoever they can."

Her voice came out hoarse and weak. "On it." She ran to Craig's truck. It seemed far away. Heat surged through her body as she forced her legs to pump hard, fighting against the resistance of the sand.

Yanking the door open with a creak, she hoisted herself up into the seat and grabbed the radio from the dashboard. Pushing the button, her voice came out raspy and weak. "PB station, Mission Beach Tower requesting backup."

She released the button. White noise crackled through the cab.

She tried again. "PB station, I repeat, backup needed. Now. Mission Beach Tower."

A steady voice returned her call for help. "This is Main. What type of backup?"

Her hand trembled as she pushed the button again. "Crowd control." She swallowed. "We have a dead body."

Sea Creature Lover

Strawberry curls bouncing, flip-flops click-clacking, Bailey charged down the shiny white hallway of the Scripps Institute. Her left flip-flop squeaked against the polished surface as she halted at a door.

The golden nameplate on the door declared it to be the office of Doctor G. Harley. She giggled. It was hard to believe Gannon was a *doctor.* Not that she was surprised. He'd always been a brainiac. But it seemed like only yesterday she was wrestling him into the sand at the beach, tormenting him with threats of tickles.

She sighed.

He didn't like to go out and play in the water. She could only remember one time that he swam with her, the day she turned twelve. He had a sour look on his face the whole time. Yet, he wouldn't hesitate to jump on a boat, careen to the wide-open ocean, and dive into its depths in whatever latest contraption the institute had concocted for him and his fellow researchers. While her passion was, or *had been,* playing in the waves, his was with the creatures that lived in the deep below.

She rapped on the door. Shuffling came from the other side. The knob turned; the door opened. Gannon stood, copper curls disheveled, round spectacles sitting crooked on his face.

A pop interrupted her giggling as she slid a bright red lollipop from her mouth. "How long you been holed up in here?" She ran her tongue along the sticky cherry remnants across her lips.

He glanced at his watch. "Uh…dunno…"

"Let me guess. You got here at six this morning. Haven't left since."

"Uh…yeah." He looked sheepishly at his feet.

"I'd bet you haven't eaten a thing."

"Sure, I have." Gannon scanned the office.

Bailey peered past him. A half-empty Styrofoam cup, chewed around the edges, was the only thing in sight. She held up a plastic bag dangling from her fingertips. "I brought you sustenance."

"Thanks." He turned and walked over to the other side of a solid, birch desk. Shuffling papers, he stacked them to the side. "I didn't know you were stopping by today."

"Neither did I." Bailey plunked the plastic bag onto the wood desk. "Caught a ride with one of the lifeguards stationed at La Jolla." She opened the bag and pulled out a Styrofoam container.

"Oh." He scratched his head. "How will you get back then?"

She shrugged. "Probably skate back." She pointed to her shoulder bag.

"I'd offer to drive you, but I've got this deadline."

"Why am I not surprised? Haven't heard from you in several days. Figured you were holed up in here, working on some paper about the breeding habits of the giant squid, and how they lay their eggs on the ocean floor. Giant babies, three feet long, hatch in great swarms."

Gannon laughed. "Very funny. Giant squid babies are *not* three feet long."

"Really? They're tiny, like normal babies?"

"Well, not exactly. They're the size of a normal adult squid. Five to thirteen inches." Gannon reached for the Styrofoam container and opened it. The room filled with the aroma of refried beans and melted cheese. His eyes widened. "Is this…Roberto's?"

"You bet. Your favorite. Carnitas." She smiled, then slid the lollipop back in her mouth. Her cheeks caved in as she sucked the sweet candy.

Gannon rummaged through the plastic bag. "You're too nice to me."

"I know. But you're my only friend."

"That's not true. What about your surfing friends?"

She shrugged. "We've drifted apart. They're only my friends if I actually surf."

"How long's it been?"

"Dunno." She licked the cherry bulb.

"You should really get back out there. You love it."

Dammit. Why did he know her so well? And why did he always have to be right? "Meh. Too busy."

"I haven't had Roberto's in…well, I don't know how long."

"'Cause you never leave this office. Last time you came down to Mission Beach was my birthday."

His eyebrows caved in around his round spectacles. "Huh. I guess you're right."

"You should really take a day off, come and hang out. Get some sunshine. Fresh air."

He ruffled through the bag, retrieving a plastic fork and knife, and a wad of thin, paper napkins. "Yeah, maybe. Too much to do here."

"Your sea creatures would be fine without you for one day." She walked around the desk over to the glass window spanning the office.

The view was incredible. Cotton ball clouds dotted the ultramarine sky. The ocean stretched out in every direction, open, vast, unending. The lemon sun glimmered a plethora of diamonds over the aqua water. A longing ran through her. When was the last time she'd been out, past the wake, in the open ocean? Jagged rocks ran along the beach below. Sea lions slithered over them, looking for the perfect perch to sun their bodies.

She turned back to Gannon. "There's more sea lions than usual, no?"

Gannon chewed vigorously on a massive bite of carnitas, melted cheese sticking to the side of his mouth. He gulped down the bite. "Yeah. There are. It's pupping season. They herd ashore. The mothers spend days out at sea feeding, then come in to nurse."

"Where do the males go?"

"North. To feeding grounds." Gannon piled charred pork, melted cheese and fresh guacamole onto a ripped chunk of tortilla, then shoved it into his mouth.

Bailey slid the lollipop from her mouth, eyeballing the dwindling piece of candy. "Geez. It's like you haven't eaten in a week. Don't you ever feed yourself? You'll be no good to your precious sea animals if you die of starvation."

He shook his head, concentrating on his next bite.

Bailey sat down at the desk, across from him.

Gannon dropped the fork and knife into the container. He slapped his forehead with his palm. "Oh. Can't believe I forgot. Guess I was depleted."

"Forgot what?" Bailey raised an eyebrow.

Wiping his hands with several of the thin napkins, he stood and leaned over the desk. He shuffled through a stack of papers, pulled one from the pile, then snapped it down on the desk. "You *must* have heard about this." The headline read "Woman Killed by Fanged Sea Monster."

Bailey bit down on the small remainder of the cherry lollipop, crunching the tiny shards against her teeth. "Uh…yeah. I was there."

"You were there?" Gannon shoved the Styrofoam container aside. He unfolded the paper and spread it out. He stood, looking down at the article, running his finger along the words.

"Yeah. It's kind of why I dropped in. I was skating along the boardwalk. There was a huge crowd, gathered by the shore. There were three lifeguard trucks, and a police cruiser. I stopped, went over to see what was going on." Her muscles tensed. "Figured someone had a run-in with a big wave." She swallowed, hard. "But…well…"

"You saw the woman?"

"Yeah." Explicit photos plastered the page throughout the article. "Why would they include these pictures?"

"Probably some journalist wormed his way in before the police showed up. It isn't exactly the highest-class paper."

Gannon pointed at the title on the top of the page. The *San Diego Sneaker.*

"It's a trashy press. They're always posting lies about the bands that come through. Accusing them of playing the Devil's music." Bailey rolled her eyes.

Staring at the photos of the puncture wounds, she could still feel that scaly fin scraping against her skin, the last day she saw Braydon. They had all told her she'd imagined it. That there hadn't been anything scabrous slithering through the water. Ransacking her brain, she searched for the memory of the marks on his leg. Something had bitten him leaving three cylindrical puncture wounds. That, she was sure of. They had looked exactly like the holes cluttering this dead woman's legs and arms. *Dammit.*

Gannon ran his finger down the page, halting, digging his pointer into the paper. "Fang-like bite marks in several places along the woman's legs and shoulder."

"I saw them. Sets of three holes. Filled with blood." Bailey fought against the wave of images rushing through her mind, reminding her of the bite marks piercing Braydon's flesh.

"And this…" Gannon searched the article again, spouting off more words. "An unbearable stench emanated from the woman's body. Did you smell this odor?"

"I did." Bailey gagged at the memory. "Seriously, Gannon, it was gross. Like a dead sea animal, washed ashore for days, picked apart by sea birds." She swallowed back the bile crawling up her throat. "I'd rather not think about it again."

"Well, maybe the woman had been dead a while. But then why didn't she wash up on the beach? It's all strange. What could have possibly done this? They think she was swimming. There weren't any boats or boards or anything around. What would lurk that close to shore?"

"She could have been past the wake." Bailey remembered the peaceful moments on her board, waiting for the next wave.

"True. Good swimming on the other side, especially in the evening. But even then. The only things out there are dolphins. The occasional shark comes in that close. But, a shark bite, that wouldn't look anything like these holes." He reinspected the newspaper. "Shark would take off half her arm, at least." He scratched his head.

"Last time there was a shark attack…geez… That was at least a year ago, wasn't it?"

"Almost. Last July. It was weird. Tiger shark. They don't usually attack humans. This one came in further than usual, looking for food. The shellfish level had gone down drastically that year."

Bailey asked, "So, what has three long teeth?"

Gannon discarded the article. "Good question." He faced the computer on his desk and started typing. "I've been digging into the Scripps database. Look at this."

Bailey walked to the other side of the desk and hovered behind him.

A silver-grey fish with round, black eyes flashed on the screen. Two massive fangs sprouted upwards from the bottom lip, sliding into holes in the upper part of the mouth.

"Oh God."

"The payara fish. Also known as the vampire fish." Gannon sighed. "Fangs are large enough to have made those holes in that woman. Problem is, it only has *two* larger fangs. The rest of its teeth pale in comparison." He pointed at rows of much smaller teeth lining the rest of the mouth.

Gannon clicked the mouse and typed some more. Another fish sprung to life on the screen. This one looked more like a sea monster. Black skin lined with mounds of white flesh stretched over a large body. Its mouth, a black cavern, covered half its face. Its teeth, clear and glassy, protruded in pairs. Two from its upper mouth, and two from the bottom. They intertwined, meeting in a quadruple of sharp sheers.

"Four teeth," Bailey said, her hand covering her mouth.

"Yeah. Four. Not three." Gannon ran his hands wildly through his hair. "The fangtooth. Its teeth are so long, they slide into pouches in the roof of its mouth to prevent them from piercing its brain. It's one of the deepest living fish. Lives in the bathyal zone. It's been found as deep as five thousand meters."

"The swimmer..." The menacing fangs almost sprung from the screen.

"The swimmer wouldn't have been deep enough to encounter a fangtooth."

"Does it ever come up?"

"Diel migration. At night, it migrates up to shallower water to feed. But...not above five hundred meters below, as far as we know. And they usually stick to the Gulf of Mexico." Gannon threw his hands up in the air. "I don't get it. I only scratched the surface on the database, but I put in key terms. If there was something that had three fangs of this length, it would have shown up."

"Or you would know about it. With all your years of research."

"Maybe. There's a lot we don't know about the depths of the ocean. The research community suspects there are *many* species that we have yet to discover. These fish that I showed you, they're only wild guesses of what could have bitten that woman."

Bailey grabbed the paper and stared at the photos of the dead woman. The three blood caverns piercing the flesh stuck in Bailey's mind. The odor materialized in her nostrils as if she were standing on the beach, staring down at the corpse again. She couldn't get past the thought churning through her head that those were the same bites that had killed Braydon.

She shook off the shiver chilling her skin.

720 Beach House

The 720 in *720 Beach House* had been scratched out. 666 had been carved crudely in its place. Bailey shook her head and took a long drag from her joint. People freaked out when they suspected the music of the Devil was being played at the beachside joint. Metal wasn't evil. It was the ultimate high. Besides, most of the shows here were hard rock, barely reaching into the realms of metal.

She snubbed out her joint on the bottom of her platinum boot and slid it into the pocket of her leather jacket. The black door swung easily on old hinges as she pulled it open and walked into the dive club.

Body odor and booze invaded her nostrils. She took a deep breath, relishing in the smell of raw life. Bailey strode up to the bar and leaned against it. A tanned, muscular young man on the other side of the gritty counter-top cluttered in carvings and graffiti saw her and walked up,

"Usual?" He winked at her. His soft brown waves framed his baby face.

"Sure, Johnny." She smiled. He was cute and always flirted with her. But he wasn't her type. He was too…clean.

He set a shot glass on the counter and poured Jack Daniel's to the brim. After pulling a can of Cali Creamin' from a fridge, he set it on the counter. The tab opened with a snap, followed by a hiss.

Bailey slid a bill over the counter. "Keep the change." She batted her eyelashes.

Certain the playfulness between them was simply a little fun between friends, she loved that he watched out for her when she came to a show.

"When did the mark of the Devil get scratched over the door?" she asked.

Johnny shook his head and tossed a white bar towel over his shoulder. "Must have been last night. We'll have to have it sanded and repainted."

"Stupid losers."

"Hey, new band tonight. First time playing here." Johnny settled his elbows on the bar.

"Raw Sugar. They're new on the circuit. First tour." Bailey took a swig of the beer. Vanilla danced over her tongue.

"I'm sure you saw the flyer."

"Of course."

"They look rough."

Bailey smirked. "You think anyone that isn't clean-cut like you is rough. Yet, you survive in this joint just fine." She tilted the can to her lips.

A shout came from the other end of the bar. "Restless bunch. I'll catch up with you later."

"You better. Don't miss my next round." She eyeballed the Jack Daniel's waiting for her on the countertop.

"I wouldn't dare." He departed to attend to the impatient patrons.

Without the distraction of flirting with Jonny, the fresh memory of the dead woman on the beach materialized. The ghastly images of her contorted limbs and the bloody wounds in her flesh clung to Bailey's mind. Wrapping her pointer and thumb around the shot glass, she tilted her head back in a smooth motion and downed the alcohol. Sweet oak burned the back of her tongue and slid down her throat. A hint of a buzz started to numb her mind, distracting her from thoughts of something lurking in the ocean.

She grabbed her beer then crawled her eyes across the room. No one interesting had shown up yet. It was early still, but she liked to get here in time for a few drinks before the crowd thickened, preparing herself for the first glimpse of the band. Entrance was everything.

After another round, and continuous scanning of the night's crowd, she made her way over to the black door and swung it open. The fresh sea air dotted her face. She closed her eyes and breathed deeply. The setting sun cast a tangerine-pink glow over the white-blue ocean. The odd star sparkled a meek hello. She loved this place and refused to leave. Even now, after a terrifying reminder of the day that Braydon died, she wouldn't flee, no matter what was out there in her beloved ocean.

Bailey pulled the half-finished joint from her leather jacket pocket along with a lighter. As she clicked the wheel to light the flame, she stared at the bold lettering engraved in the cheap plastic. Devil's Tongue. The night she'd purchased the band swag had been a fun one. A shiver hijacked her as she pictured the lavish blond tresses and piercing green eyes of the lead singer.

She snapped her attention back to the joint and lit it. The pink hues of the horizon turned a burnt orange as she took a long drag.

An electric chord vibrated through the black door, grabbing her attention. Had to be showtime. Probably a couple of minutes for some roadie to finish the sound check, but it wouldn't be long.

She took one last drag, dropped the butt on the ground, and stamped it out.

Another round was overdue.

The stuffy heat rising from the growing number of bodies moistened her skin as she re-entered the bar. Johnny saw her heading toward him and got to work. Another shot glass full of oaky deliciousness and a vanilla cream ale waited for her when she reached him. She winked at Johnny, slid him a bill, then shot back the JD. Bailey grabbed the beer, then hovered at the back of the room. The perfect place to inspect her prey.

A scrawny kid in ripped jeans and a tattered Raw Sugar t-shirt worked frantically over the stage, checking mics and strumming guitars. The show would start any minute.

Halfway into her beer, the lights dimmed. Purple lighting glowed over the stage. Burt, the bar owner, stumbled up to the main microphone. He bellowed, "Is everyone ready?"

The crowd yelled out an enthusiastic, drunken rumble.

Burt repeated, "I said, are you ready?"

Whistles and screeches erupted through the tightly packed space.

Burt concluded his introduction. "Let's hear it for Raw Sugar." He stumbled back off the stage.

The purple lights glowed brighter, then blended into a red-orange hue. Electricity jolted through the room as the strums of a gritty guitar riff vibrated through the air. Through Bailey's extremities. She chugged the rest of her beer. Her buzz increased to an acceptable level.

His timing ever perfect, Johnny slid another beer and shot glass her way. She set the empty can on the bar and passed Johnny a couple of bills. He rushed away to deal with a sudden influx of patrons.

After gulping back the JD, she slipped a small mirror from the inside pocket of her jacket and made a quick check of her appearance. Her wild curls remained teased and hair-sprayed into place. Midnight eyeshadow lay in thick layers, masquerading her eyes into deep mysteries. Her lips, thick with cherry red gloss, remained smooth and ready. She slid the mirror back into her jacket pocket and downed a third of the beer. Perfect. She'd be a mess by the end of the show, anyway, coated in sweat and glistening in a rock 'n' roll bath.

The guitar riff had heightened. The man behind the instrument made his way through the red-orange hue, now turning to a purple-blue. Black pleather stretched over the muscular contours of his legs. His face hid behind a long, full mane of wild extremes. Electricity pumped through the air in response as his fingers strummed his guitar. The drunken crowd awoke, screaming in anticipation. As she swallowed another third of the beer, Bailey's insides fluttered in anticipation.

An edgy voice, laced with a pure rock 'n' roll vibe, pulsated through the room. Bailey closed her eyes and let the music take over her body. When the song reached the chorus, she re-opened her eyes and scanned the lead man standing in the center of the stage. Long, splendid waves of golden hair fell over his shoulders, framing his young yet rough and chiseled face. His eyes wandered over the crowd, speaking of experience.

A cosmic haze of color illuminated his silhouette as he moved across the stage and broke out in a ferocious cry. Pleather encased his muscular legs. A red shirt, buttons open down to his torso, exposed his tanned, smooth chest. Metal rings dotted his fingers. Leather bracelets wove up the sides of his arms. Sweat trickled down his chest.

Bailey had an urge to walk right up to him and lick the droplets off his body. Electric thrills sizzled her veins. Her body buzzed.

She downed the remaining beer, set it on the bar, then fluffed up her hair. It was time. She weaved her way through the tightly packed crowd, sliding between exuberant, drunken patrons, keeping her eyes glued to the rock god.

Reaching the edge of the stage, her body became one with the music. Her eyes slithered their way up his rugged body, finding his coffee eyes. Satisfied with her prey, every part of her sunk into the toxic mix of guitar vibes and aggressive vocals. She stared up at the source of the intoxicating voice, waiting for him to notice her.

His eyes continued exploring the crowd. Until they found her. Inspecting her, his gaze ran up her legs, over her breasts, then met hers. Her body eased, grinding out exaggerated, sensual movements, matching the rhythm of his voice as it heightened. His face glistened under the glare of the stage lights. She licked her lips. The crowd faded from her mind.

He snapped his gaze away, throwing his head back, howling at new heights. As the song ended, the crowd erupted, and the heat in the room intensified.

Bailey perused the rock god that would be hers. The night was young and already it was exactly what she needed to drown out the dead body on the beach and the creature in the ocean.

Sea Panic

Bailey blasted down the boardwalk, the sea breeze whipping through her curls. She breathed in the salty air and toyed with the cherry lollipop in her mouth, swirling it around with her tongue. The wheels on her roller skates click-clacked in rhythm, cruising over the long, open boardwalk. On a weekday, there were less people to dodge. She could skate fast and feel free.

Reaching the end of the cul-de-sac near 720 Beach House, she eased to a slow roll. The pier stretched out into the ocean off Pacific Beach. A cruise down to the end would be nice. There were almost always dolphins playing out there.

A horn blared, jolting her attention. Gannon hung out of his Jeep, waving his hands wildly, shouting, "Bailey. Bailey."

She rolled her eyes. He could be so dramatic. What was he doing down here, anyway?

She rolled over to his Jeep and up to his head hanging out of the window and pulled the lollipop from her lips with a pop. "What are you doing here?"

"Something happened."

A tremor contorted her muscles. The memory of the dead body on the beach materialized. "What do you mean?"

"The bite marks. On the woman…"

"The woman who washed up on Mission Beach?"

"Get in. I'll show you."

She hesitated. Those bite marks were way too familiar. Did she really want to know where they came from?

"Bailey, just get in." He scowled.

"Okay. Okay. Easy turbo." She rolled over to the passenger side, opened the door, and hoisted herself up.

She'd barely closed the door when Gannon pressed his foot to the gas. The Jeep surged. Her head jerked back against the headrest. "Gannon, seriously?"

"Be quiet. You'll understand. Once you see it."

Jesus Christ. What the hell is going on? First a corpse on the beach, then a new rock god in town, and now Gannon all wired up. Her world was spinning out of control.

Sea Lion

Gannon pulled the Jeep into a stall in the staff parking lot at the back of the Scripps Institute. He jammed the brakes on, and Bailey jostled forward. She glared at him, then released her seatbelt, opened the door, and eased herself out. The wheels on her roller skates met the pavement and she rolled over to the driver's side with ease.

Gannon jumped down, locked the door, then looked at her, his face grey and pale. "C'mon." He walked briskly across the parking lot, heading for the institute.

Bailey rolled behind him.

"You got a change of footwear in your bag?"

"Yeah, of course." Bailey always carried a pair of flip-flops. A spontaneous stop for a quick one at 720 was always a possibility.

"You should change then. We're going down the stairs." Gannon motioned at a bench in front of the entranceway.

Bailey sat, slipped off her shoulder bag, fished out her flip-flops, then untied her skates.

Gannon hovered over her.

"Stop glaring at me. You're making me nervous."

"Yeah, well, I'm in a hurry. I don't really have time for all this. My paper is due. I have another set of data to plow through." He ran his hands through his hair in manic motions. "And now this."

Bailey slipped her flip-flops on and dropped each roller skate into the bag. "And now what?"

"I'll show you." He took off.

She followed, half running to keep up. The flip-flop on her left foot snapped back, almost blowing out. She fumbled as she adjusted it, then jogged to catch up. *What's with Gannon? Why this sudden panic?*

He swiped his access card, the door clicked, then he opened it and held it for her. Once she was in, he released it, and the door clicked shut behind them. He darted down a long hallway. She could barely keep up. He swiped his card again, opened another door, then proceeded down a staircase. She grabbed the railing and followed cautiously. Wide gaps in the steel steps revealed a dreary, industrial-looking room below.

"Wow. You've never taken me down here before," she said.

He looked over his shoulder, continuing a manic pace. "You're not supposed to be down here. But I need to show you this."

"What, Gannon? Show me what?"

"This." He halted in front of a six-foot, steel cylinder. A small, circular window housed the middle of the smooth body.

"What is this? A submarine?"

"No. Submarines are for the military. This is a DVS. Deep submergence vehicle."

"You research dudes go down into the ocean in this thing?"

"Yes. It's a knockoff of the Alvin."

"The Alvin?"

"State of the art DVS. The only one purely devoted to deep ocean research. Anyway, when they built the Alvin, they cut three cylinders. First two were prototypes. Steel isn't as high-grade as the final version. This one was donated to Scripps. Good enough for our ventures. Not as durable as the Alvin."

"So why did you bring me down here? You could get in trouble."

"I know." Gannon scanned the room nervously.

"It's not like you to break rules." She nudged him with her elbow.

"I had no choice." He grabbed her hand, pulling her to the front of the marine vehicle. "A team went out a couple of days ago. Air samples from out at the Scripps Pier showed some unusual gases in high amounts. They were tracking further out, trying to determine where the gases came from. Whether or not they were seeping up from below the surface. Apparently, they were about seven hundred meters down when it happened." He continued pulling her by the hand, around to the front of the cylinder. Another window at the nose of the vehicle allowed them to peer into the internals of the deep-water machine.

"When what happened?" Her heart pattered as her thoughts raced back to the moment she laid eyes on the dead woman on the beach.

"This." He pulled her around the other side, halted, and stared at the steel.

There were three holes in the metal, just below the third window. Punctures, in the steel. She put her hand over her mouth. "You don't think…"

"I didn't think it was possible. The bite marks in the woman that washed ashore, they went nearly four inches into her flesh, according to the medical examiner. At least that's what was quoted in the paper. I measured the holes in the Sea Lion." He paused, staring at the punctures in the metal.

"The Sea Lion?"

"Yeah. It's what the team named the craft. The holes match. I still don't believe it, but why are they exactly the same size as the ones in the woman? And why three?"

Bailey stared at the holes in disbelief. It couldn't be. The same thing that had bitten that woman could bite through steel? No. "What is this thing made of?"

"Steel. HY-80. Fifty-millimeter-thick plates of it. Not as hefty as the titanium hull of the Alvin, which was originally HY-90 steel and then upgraded to titanium in 1973 so they could go deeper." He shook his head, running his hands through his hair again. "Still, it should be too strong for a fish to pierce with its teeth."

Bailey stared at the Sea Lion. Goosebumps ran over her arms. A ball of instinct curled around her gut. Was she ready to face what had happened to Braydon? To face her fear of the deep water?

Gannon's voice broke her thoughts. "I wouldn't have even measured them, or been suspicious, but the two researchers that were in the Sea Lion when this happened…well, they said they saw a flash of purple, fluorescent light. That some horrible smell seeped into the cabin inside, and then they heard a crunch. After that…nothing. The light vanished. The odor receded. They got the hell back here and didn't even realize the metal had been punctured until they parked the Sea Lion, got out, and walked around the exterior."

Bailey stared at Gannon, imagining two scrawny men with doctorates out in the middle of the nowhere, surrounded by water. "They were lucky."

Gannon nodded. "They were. If the punctures had gone through to the other side, then the air pressure could have been compromised."

Bailey slid her backpack off, unzipped it, and pulled out a fresh lollipop. She zipped it back up, slid the bag over her shoulder, unwrapped the candy, and popped it into her mouth.

He side-eyed her. "Those are bad for your teeth, you know?"

"Whatever." She sucked on the cherry candy, wondering what the hell the punctures meant and what she was supposed to do about it. "So, what now?"

"I don't know. I told them we need to report this to the authorities. That it might be linked to whatever attacked that woman."

"And?"

"They think I'm crazy. They said the purple glow was from the algae, the odor from the gases they were tracking, and the punctures... They're convinced they scraped a rock."

"Really?"

"Yeah. They suspect I'm cuckoo."

Anxiety clawed at her gut as the memories of the aftermath from the accident flooded her mind. She could still hear herself repeating her words over and over, describing the holes in Braydon's leg, the purple light, the smell...she could still see all those faces looking back at her like she was some sort of maniac. "I know how you feel." She put her hand on Gannon's shoulder. "I believe you. But I don't know what we're supposed to do about it."

Gannon frowned. "Wait until someone else dies, I guess."

Wave House

With perfect balance, Bailey ascended the large white wave and rode the aqua peak. Ocean misted wind danced with her hair.

She spun her board down and plunged into the deep. Underneath, the world became quiet. She stared into the watery depths as she took several long, hard strokes. A burst of bubbles obscured her vision.

Then a shadow crossed her path.

With a large gasp, she broke to the surface and gulped in air. Rather than the shoreline spanning out for miles in both directions, a deck dotted with boards and tanned bodies came into view. Completely lost in the moment, she'd forgotten she was riding an artificial wave and not out in the ocean. The shadow beneath the water must have been a figment of her imagination. She searched for her board, but it was nowhere in sight. She paddled over to the edge and slid onto the sunbathed deck. There she spotted one of her old surfing buddies, Dalton, her board under his arm, walking her way. If she was into clean-cut surfer types, she would have eaten him up. Besides not being her type, she refused to let physical attraction interfere with a friendship.

She stood on the deck and inspected the makeshift wave, appearing so lifelike. The Wave House was the only place she knew of that had a state-of-the-art machine to simulate the movement of the ocean's wake. Positioned next to the boardwalk, it housed the best patio with a sandy beach floor, picnic tables, and cheap booze. All the seasoned wave riders hung out here.

Twice a week at minimum, Bailey practiced her moves on the fake waves. Past the boardwalk, the ocean opened, vast and unending, calling to her. She couldn't respond. Refusing to relive the last time she'd paddled over the wake, mounted her board, and summitted a beautiful, white wave, she'd suppressed the memory. She didn't want to face how free she'd been, careening for the shore, side by side with Braydon. The day she'd lost him, she'd stopped surfing and destroyed a piece of herself. She wanted it back but was too afraid to face her suppressed emotions.

"Hey, Bailey," Dalton's deep voice greeted her.

He sported surfing shorts and nothing else. His muscles rippled under his tanned skin and his sunbathed baby face glistened with tanning oil and sweat from the heat. Welcoming her with a wide smile he said, "Here's your board. It popped out the back."

"Thanks." She took the board, rested the back tip on the pavement, and leaned an elbow over the top. The shiny blue tinted with silver streaks glimmered under the bright sun. It was her favorite board—a birthday gift from Braydon. But that was years ago, before the accident. She still had the board, but Braydon was gone.

"Nice run," Dalton said.

"It felt good."

"Wish you'd go out with me sometime." He peered out at the ocean.

The pavement warmed her bare feet. "I don't know."

"Hey, wanna beer?" He nodded over to the picnic tables dotting the sandy ground.

"Sure." She'd love a cold one. Especially if it got him off the topic of surfing in the ocean.

Luscious Obsidian

Bailey peered into the mirror, contemplating the sadness in her eyes. Running into Dalton reminded her of how much she loved coasting to the shore, her curls tangled and salty, her skin glistening in the sun. After digging bits of sand out from under her nails and rinsing them under the tap, she fluffed her hair a few times then headed for the door. The notion of a cold, cream ale taunted her.

Spotting Dalton at a table, she walked over to him and set her board against the fence.

"Bailey," Dalton exclaimed. "Sit. I ordered you a beer."

A cream ale had been set at an open spot at the picnic table. Several other surfer types, none of whom she recognized, lined the sides of the table.

"Hi. I'm Jim," one guy said.

"Tom," another said.

The last man glanced her way. "Jan."

They were clones—blond hair, tanned skin, muscular, surfing shorts, and not much else. Placing her shoulder bag on the bench near the cream ale, she sat next to Jan. The first sip of the cold drink refreshed her parched throat.

Normally, she wouldn't sit with a group of cookie-cutter surfers. But she missed Braydon and needed a distraction from the horrifying event on the beach.

Chatter broke out around the table as talk of surfing exploded. It was inevitable.

About a third of the way into her beer, she spun around on the picnic table bench and scanned the crowd. As usual, the place was drowning in surfers. She loved being on her board, dancing with a wave. The peacefulness of it all pulled her in. But when it came to talk of board dimensions, waxes, styles, and moves, her eyes glazed over. Surfers understood that feeling of perching on the peak of a wave, out in the ocean, just you and the water. However, they could get on her nerves awfully quick with all their tech talk. The purity of riding a wave stirred her passion, not the latest and greatest board.

Scanning the clones in surf shorts, she took another drink. A glimmer caught her eye. Three guys mingled under the archway of the Wave House entrance.

A slight gasp escaped from her lips.

The leader of the group was unlike anything she'd ever laid eyes on. He was tall. His stark straight hair fell in long, obsidian strands, fanning around his shoulders and fluttering across his chiseled face. A silky shirt, opened down to his torso, shot shimmers off under the glare of the sun. Tight jeans clung to his muscular legs.

He was definitely not a surfer. He looked like he belonged at 720 Beach House, belting out a rock tune.

Tingles ran down her arms. Maybe he was in town for a show. She didn't recall seeing his photo on any of the flyers. Although, some of the bands simply printed their logos or an album cover.

She explored him with her eyes. After a few moments, he started walking across the sand. His entourage followed him to a table at the back.

"Hey, earth to Bailey. Want another round?" Dalton's voice ended her stalking.

"Sure." She pretended to join in the surfer talk. Every few seconds, she stole a glance over to the table where Obsidian Hair had led his group. This time his dark eyes caught hers, but she couldn't look away. She froze.

He didn't look her up and down, just held her gaze for what seemed to be a really long time. Heat flushed through her.

Dalton set another cream ale on the table, then proceeded to deliver beers to the rest of his friends.

"Thanks." She smiled at him.

He grinned. "No problem. You seem spaced out."

"Nah. Just tired."

Dalton returned to his seat and settled back into the discussion.

She wanted to look again but knew she shouldn't. Then, she did. He was engaged in discussion with his friends. She longed to touch his luscious hair. He shot a look her way and caught her staring again. This time, he smiled, and when he did, her insides melted. Her cheeks blazed.

Bailey. What are you doing?

She focused on the conversation. Dalton's friends were standing, making their exit.

"Listen, I gotta run. It was really nice running into you," Dalton said. "You wanna ride?"

She looked at her beer. Obsidian hair swept through her mind. "No. I'll hang for a bit."

"You sure? You okay?"

"I'm fine. I'm just gonna chill. Might do another run."

"All right. If you change your mind about surfing, for real, let me know." He nodded.

"Yeah. Sure." She watched Dalton walk over to the exit then stared at her beer, doubting she'd ever surf with him again.

"Mind if I join you?" someone said.

She looked up. Obsidian hair stood over her. A mist of vanilla floated from him. "Sure," she said.

He produced a cream ale and placed it in front of her as he sat down. "I noticed what you were drinking. Figured if you let me join you, I shouldn't come empty-handed." His deep, rich voice soothed her.

"Thanks." She shot back the rest of her half-drunk beer, put it aside, and grabbed the fresh one.

He sat next to her, his thigh almost touching hers. "I'm Rhys."

She swallowed. Her voice came out meek. "I'm Bailey."

As he settled beside her, she took a deep breath, willing herself to relax.

She arched her eyebrow. "You're not from around here, are you?"

"No. First time here."

"You're not a surfer."

He examined his attire. "No. That I am not. As you can see. We're in town for a show."

"720?"

"Yeah. You hang out there?"

She nodded. "Never miss a show."

"Then you'll be there for ours." He took a long pull from his beer.

"Depends. What do you play?"

He set the beer on the table, his muscles bulging under the sleeves of his shirt. "Sometimes we cover Zeppelin, Aerosmith, GN'R. We've been playing more of our own, though. Just released our first album."

"Really? What's the title?"

"*Anarchy.*"

It sounded badass. "Nice. Band name?"

"Angels of Death."

"Double nice." She took a swig of beer. "Where you from?"

"L.A. We've been hitting all the dirty dives there. Finally packed it into our van, and we're doing the coast, then heading cross country."

"Big time."

"Oh yeah. Months on end holed up in a shitty van with those filthy assholes." He nodded over to his bandmates. They raised their beers in a raucous toast. "You're from here?" he asked.

"Yeah. Lifeguard by day." *Party animal by night.*

"You surf?" He nodded at her board.

"Not really." She blushed. "I mean, I did. I used to. Now I stick to the waves here." She stared at the fake waves belting from the machine. A chunky dude in loose shorts bailed.

"Woah. Big spill." Rhys switched his attention back to her. "So you quit?"

"You could say that." She focused on her beer can, fumbling her fingers over it. "Say, you drink anything other than that?" She tilted her can to his.

"Yeah. Jack Daniels is a friend of mine."

Had she just met a rock angel? Bailey waved at a waitress crossing the sand. "Could we get another round, and two shots of JD?"

The waitress nodded, then walked over to the bar.

"Since you're from out of town, I'll show you some local hospitality." The sea breeze played with her hair.

"I appreciate that." He set his beer on the table and pulled a brightly colored flyer from his jeans pocket. Unfolding it, he smoothed it out and slid it across the table. "Our show. So you don't miss it."

She took the paper and scrutinized it. The cover art was fantastic, a lethal mix of devil horns, fire, and long-haired rock gods with evil seething from their eyes. "Nice cover."

"So, you'll come? To the show?"

She folded the flyer and slipped it into her shoulder bag. "Sure."

The waitress returned with two shot glasses filled to the brim with sweet liquor and placed them on the table, then added two beers alongside—a Cali Creamin' and a Green Flash.

Rhys slipped a hand into his pocket, pulling out a bill.

"No. I insist. San Diego hospitality." Bailey put a hand over his. Electricity shot through her fingers.

He smiled.

Bailey fished through her shoulder bag and retrieved a couple of bills. She handed them to the waitress.

"Nice of you," he said.

"San Diegans are nice. You owe me one hell of a show."

"Now that I can do." He picked up the shot glass. "Here's to the Devil's music."

"I'll drink to that." She picked up the other shot glass, tipped it his way, then downed the liquid.

Duty Calls

The beach reached for miles upon miles in both directions like a blanket woven of tiny sparkling glass granules. Waves rolled in and crashed, dissipating into watery fingers that stretched over the hard-packed sand dotted in broken seashells and shattered bits of seaweed. The fresh sea breeze kissed her skin as Bailey reclined against the high seat and extended her legs. Up here, on her guard's throne, she watched the section of Pacific Beach under her care. At least until Craig arrived to relieve her.

Seagulls squealed. Kids giggled. Moms scolded the adventurous ones for disobeying the rules and going too far out. A small black-haired boy worked on a sloppy project somewhat resembling a sandcastle. He pulled a bright blue pail upward, wet sand pouring out in globs as it stuck to his fingers. He studied his sludge-covered appendages in awe, as if he couldn't understand what had happened to his masterpiece.

Bailey chuckled.

A scream pierced the air.

Bailey sat up straight, quickly scanning the shore, then seeking the source of the intrusion along the water's surface. Another scream. A teenager screeched, "Stop it," pulling her tiny bikini top over her adolescent breasts. A lanky tanned teenager with sun-bleached hair grabbed her and pulled her under the water.

Bailey shook her head and resumed her steady watch.

A surfer perched atop a wave as it rolled in. He crested a white cap, then eased down the other side. He slid into the water in a smooth motion, his board popping up, then his head. How long had it been since she'd been out there, past the wake? She knew but didn't want to admit it. The feel of her board under her feet wasn't the same at the Wave House. A longing throbbed in her gut.

A cry violated her ears. Louder and more desperate than the sounds of the teenagers engaged in horseplay, it grabbed her gut. She stood, used her palm as a makeshift sun shield, and inspected the horizon in a smooth shot.

"Help!" The high-pitched squeal halted Bailey's search.

"Oh, dear God. Help him," a woman cried. Bailey quickly scoured the shoreline.

A woman in a one-piece aqua bathing suit designed to flatter a body that had once produced children waved at her then pointed out into the ocean.

Bailey's eyes followed the woman's arm out across the white-capped surface. Everything appeared normal. Bikini-clad tanned bodies floated and swam.

"Oh my god," the woman yelled. She stared up at Bailey, slapping her palms on either side of her face.

Bailey jumped from the highchair, sand scattering as her feet hit the beach. She grabbed a fire engine red circular flotation device hooked to the lifeguard stand, clipped the rope hanging from it to the belt across her waist, then sprinted across the sand to the woman.

The woman's eyes seeped panic. "Out there." She pointed again.

Bailey followed the instruction and surveyed far out, past the wake. A head bobbed in rhythm with the lull of the ocean. Small arms flailed, hands hitting the water, throwing splashes askew. The next wave in the steady wake rolled in, obscuring the boy behind its crest.

"My son. I told him not to go past the wake," the woman said. "I should have been watching him more closely." Shrill panic rose in her voice as her hands shook.

Bailey sprang into action, running into the water, her feet throwing splashes into swimmers' faces. Pushing her legs against the thigh-high water, she released the flotation device and let it trail behind her from the rope attached to her belt. She dove into the salty water depths, arms first, then stroked long, hard motions, ramping up her speed. Shooting through the water in a tight line, she neared the wake.

A shadow caught her gaze. She halted her swim, her body remaining in a sleek line, and scanned her surroundings. Nothing.

The kid's head bobbed on the other side of the wake as the next white-capped wave hovered in the distance. An image of Braydon glimmered in the aqua wall descending upon her as a flash of purple coated the surface with iridescence.

A shrill screech echoed from the direction of the boy.

Snapping into action, she stroked a strong motion, pulling her body close to the next oncoming wave. The pit of her stomach was heavy, like it had a hard rock lodged in it. Her heart palpitated as the massive roll of water loomed above then swallowed her up. The torrent pulled her down, into the deep. Sunlight faded to jade. Thick, underwater silence engulfed her.

In slow motion, her mind relived the last moments she'd spent with Braydon. Blood poured from deep holes in his flesh as panic and fear riddled his face. Another flash of light illuminated the thick aqua, forcing her back to the present moment. Bailey paddled manically, kicked wildly, and pushed her way to the surface. Gasping for air, she scoured the water frantically, unable to find the boy.

"Help," the boy screamed.

She followed his voice. His head barely bobbed above the water as he spit mouthfuls of water back into the ocean.

Something brushed Bailey's leg. She froze. *Just a fish. Or a string of algae.* The beach seemed far away.

The mom waved her arms in a frantic plea.

Bailey turned to the kid. The next wave rolled in fast. She braced herself, took the hit, then resurfaced.

"Mommy," the kid shrieked then choked as he spat up water.

The fear churning in the pit of her belly clawed through her. *No. Not now.* She gritted her teeth, stared at the struggling boy, and paddled hard. The next wave thundered, coming at her fast. She refused to let up, resurfacing, and paddling to the boy.

She grabbed him, slid the flotation device over his head, then took his hand in hers. He stared at her, wide-eyed and trembling.

"Hey, kid. Hold onto this." She placed his small hand onto the ring.

The kid nodded, his shoulders quivering, teeth chattering.

"You're with me now. I'll tow you back to your mom. Okay?"

He nodded.

Something brushed against Bailey's leg again. Something slippery, like a fin. She plunged her head into the water, looking into the depths below. A shadow crept through the dark, pulsing deep. Then nothing.

A chill ran through her. She jerked her head back and forth, scanning the surface, her hair floating in the water around her. The words "swim now" shot through her mind.

She paddled up behind the kid and grabbed the flotation device. Bailey glanced back, watching the next wave roll in. As it neared, she leaned her body into the floating ring and paddled hard with both arms. She caught the wave, riding it up in an awkward body surf, pushing the boy along in front.

He protested, but she ignored him and concentrated on the ride. They crested. A thrill shot through her, reminding her of the experience of reaching the apex of a perfect wave.

Pain pierced her shin, shooting up her leg. She jolted. Her gut seized.

Something slippery slid along her thigh.

Panic gripped her gut. She kicked hard, then guided the boy down the other side of the wave.

The kid bobbed with the soft lulling remnants of the wake. She turned her head and scanned the surface. Pain seared her shin, reaching up her leg. *What the hell?* Had something bitten her?

An image materialized in her mind, strong and bright. That day, out in the open ocean—the last day she saw Braydon. Desperation hijacked his face as she clutched onto him. Blood had seeped from the marks in his leg, staining the ocean. A massive wave had crashed over them, swallowing him. An aftermath of disbelief had followed. Pills and therapy sessions had been thrust upon her. Professionals declared that she had suffered from a fear-induced hallucination. Braydon's body hadn't been found, leaving it impossible for her to prove what she saw.

A shadow beneath the ripples grabbed her attention. Nausea swelled in her stomach. She continued to push the kid as she kicked her legs with all her might, propelling them through the water. Her shoulders contracting, her legs on fire, she kicked through the strain, through the burning, resisting the human urge to stop. She told her brain to shut up, focusing on the shoreline, the mom clasping her hands over her mouth and heart, and the crowd standing, watching in fear and awe.

The pain intensified, sending small knives up her thigh and into her abdomen. She swore that something hovered alongside her. She kicked as hard as she could in a savage motion, like a harbor seal swimming from a shark.

After a lifetime of fighting the thick water, her feet found the ocean bottom. She pulled the flotation device off the kid, letting it trail behind by the rope still attached to her belt. She scooped him up and held him tight, his legs and arms wrapping around her in desperation. She forced her way through the heavy water in a slow run, reached the shore, and put the kid down.

The woman grabbed him, suffocating him in a hug fueled by love.

Bailey surveyed the crowd. Their shocked faces stared her down. Fingers pointed at her and hands covered their mouths.

Craig ran up to her. "Bailey. Are you okay? What happened out there?" His eyes shot to her leg.

She tilted her head, pulling wet clumps of hair away from her eyes. Three holes dotted her flesh. Blood streamed down her thigh, over the beach, marking her path from the water.

In slow motion, her mind replayed the image of something hovering next to her as she swam madly to the shore. She wasn't crazy. She turned her head, finding the kid and his mom.

The mom crouched and shook her son, scolding him. "Why did you go past the wake?"

The boy's lips trembled, coated in snot and tears. "I didn't, mommy. A big fish pulled me out."

Angels of Death

Bailey swung the black door open and walked into 720 Beach House. The orange glow of the setting sun vanished. Her vision blurred as her eyes adjusted to the dim lighting. A stale scent tinged with cheap beer stamped out the fresh air lingering in her nose. She narrowed her eyes and scanned the room, trying to ignore the pain throbbing from the three holes in her thigh.

Patrons scattered, gulping back drinks before the show.

Johnny finished serving a beer. By the time she got up to the bar, he'd poured her an ample shot of Jack Daniel's and was pulling open the tab of a cream ale.

If only he wasn't so clean-cut. She sidled up to the bar and leaned against the cluttered countertop. "Thanks, Johnny." She grabbed the beer and took a swig.

"Anytime." He scanned the bar. "New band tonight."

"Yeah. They're from L.A."

"Ah. You've done some recon?" He smirked.

"A little." Nursing the beer, she tried to relax her shoulders. She shouldn't be nervous. It was just like any other night. Down a few rounds, find that sweet spot between buzzed and drunk, throw herself into the music, sweat it out with a head bang or two, eye fuck the lead singer, eat him up, then go home.

"What do you know about them?" Johnny asked.

She shook her head. "You work here. You're on shift at every live show. How is it you don't know anything about the bands that come through?" She grabbed the shot glass and threw back the sweet liquor, almost purring as the burn clawed down her throat. The potent fluid eased the churn in her stomach.

"I'm good at my job. Boss schedules me whenever it's busy. I don't like loud music. I'm only here for the tips."

"Well… Angels of Death. From L.A. First tour. Debut album." She tilted the beer can against her lips.

"Huh. Any good?"

"Don't know."

"Then how do you know so much about them?"

"Met the lead singer."

"You did?"

"He was over at the Wave House a couple of days ago. With his band." Her cheeks flamed.

"Wow. Can it be? Is Bailey blushing? You more than met him, didn't you? And now you're here. A second meeting. This is unheard of. Are you…developing feelings?"

"Shut up." She glared at him. "Nothing happened. He bought me a drink. That's all. I need a good show. And a party. I need a reason not to get out of bed tomorrow." She tossed her hair over her shoulder and turned her back to Johnny, taking a glimpse at the early arrivers.

"C'mon. I'm just playing." He pawed at the back of her leather jacket.

She turned and faced him. "I know. I just hate mushy shit."

"I know." He grabbed a bottle of Jack Daniel's and refilled her glass. "My treat. I'm sorry."

"Awww. You know the way to my heart." She grabbed the shot glass and downed the drink. Two JD in and still on her first beer. She was out of rhythm. She needed to find that easy cosmic vibe she always rode when a show started. It was proving difficult tonight. Luscious obsidian strands danced through her thoughts. Imaginary wings fluttered in her stomach. *Fuck.* What was wrong with her? She downed several large gulps of beer, trying to settle her nerves.

"Easy. You usually pace." Johnny eyeballed the empty shot glass.

"I know. I'm on edge. Don't know why."

"Everyone's on edge lately, with all the chaos on the beach. I heard what happened, yesterday. You must have been freaked." His eyes seeped with genuine concern.

"Nah. I'm fine. Part of the job. Kid could have drowned."

"Yeah, but I heard something bit you out there." He shook his head and raised his hands.

"Yeah. It was nothing. All stitched up."

"But they don't know what it was?"

"I'm sure it was just something that swam in too far." No, she wasn't. She'd seen that bite mark before, on Braydon's leg as he bobbed on the other side of the surf.

"Huh. Guess the rumors are overdone then." He didn't look convinced.

She stared into his eyes. "Listen. I'm fine. You can't believe everything you hear." Who was she trying to convince, him or herself?

"Okay. At least let me buy you a beer."

"After my heart again, are you?"

"No. I couldn't handle being used then dumped by you. Even if the sex was hot." He shook his head.

"Very funny."

A couple of guys walked up to the bar. Johnny nodded at them. "Listen, gotta do my job. I'll be back with another round. On me."

She winked at him then leaned back against the bar, facing the stage. The can in her hand was nearly empty. What could a couple of extra rounds hurt? A nice buzz would dull the images of the woman's corpse and numb the emotions surfacing as a result of the onslaught of memories of Braydon. A wild night and a day in bed was exactly what she needed.

Anarchy

Rumbles of guitar broke through the black door. The joint in her hand still had a few puffs left to offer. Usually, she liked to be at the back, against the bar, when the band made their entrance. The fluttering in her stomach refused to settle, despite the—how many?—rounds she'd tossed back. *Fuck it.* She needed any help she could get to find that psychedelic wave she loved to ride.

What was it about Rhys and his luscious, obsidian hair that had her so riled? They'd had a chill time at the Wave House. He knew his shit about music—all the greats worth talking about, anyway. Aching for a kick-ass show, she was excited about his potential to deliver.

A voice, smooth with a rough edge, rose over the sounds of the guitar. The revolt in her stomach roiled at an all-time high. She took a final, long puff. The smoke eased into her, mixing with the shots of JD—the perfect toxic cocktail.

With her free hand, she fluffed up her hair then dabbed her lips with gloss. She couldn't wait any longer to see if Angels of Death matched the imaginary show she'd played in her mind. Tossing the butt onto the concrete, she stamped it out, then swung the door open.

The flutters in her stomach turned to full-on waves. Electric vibes shot through her arms and into her core. Rhys stood center stage. A silk shirt, this time purple, flowed over his arms, open down the front, exposing his rippled chest. His mouth stretched wide as he slithered close to the microphone. A scarf woven with silver threads tied around the stand glimmered under the purple-blue haze of the stage lights. He slid his inner thigh along the stand, gyrating against it. His bare chest glistened under the lights as they turned a golden hue.

Then, the voice of a rock god rang out, descending over the entire room, from the ceiling to the floor. The voice weaved through Bailey, electrifying her brain, her arms, her legs, clutching the pit of her being. She closed her eyes. *Fuck. Yes.* She could feel him walking over the stage as his voice grew closer. The opening of the song crescendoed into an early climax. His primal screams entranced her.

She opened her eyes. There he stood. His locks fluttered around his chiseled face. The raw vibes streamed from his mouth, open wide, hovering over the steel bulb of the microphone. The crowd went wild, under his spell.

She'd heard many rock voices before, but this was different. This was the voice of a metal angel.

A fire burned through her body. Her insides raged with desire.

She snuck a look back at the bar. Johnny stood, watching the show, a cream ale and a full shot glass perched in front of him. *Perfect.* She strode up to the bar, winked at Johnny, then downed the JD. Grabbing the beer, she turned just in time to see Rhys's hair, shimmering under the fluorescent rainbow of ever-changing lights. The bass rumbled as the guitar riff climbed to a peak.

Rhys's voice reverberated through every corner of the room. The song ended, and the savage crowd screamed like a single, wild being.

The beer can was now two-thirds empty. She swigged back the last of it in three gulps. The first strums of the next song took over the room as she faced the stage.

Weaving her way through the tightly packed, sweaty bodies in a slow prowl, she devoured the metal god with her eyes. Her hunting instincts kicked in and he was her prey. Nothing would stop her now.

The set progressed. After four aggressive tracks, guitars were switched, and an acoustic set assembled in a flash. A throbbing swelled within Bailey. Even this slow ballad was tantalizing. It was the most stunning performance she'd ever seen at 720.

She undulated to the music, tuned out the noise of the crowd around her, and focused on Rhys. It was as if they were the only two in the room. Something nagged at the back of her mind, warning her. She suppressed it, stamped it out as if it didn't even exist. All she cared about in this moment was the desire building inside of her, the voice taking her to an unknown place, and the eyes pulling her in. No room. No crowd. Just her. And Rhys.

Psychedelic Ride

The room whirled. Cream bear skin blanket, purple silk sheets, diamonds flashing from a spinning ball, orange-pink lights drowned in an aqua hue, all spun into a multi-colored dream. Rhys had transformed his room in the Trade Winds Motel into a rock lover's haven. Bailey took a deep breath and tried to halt her dizziness.

Too many drinks and joints tonight had led her down an unfamiliar path of losing control.

To top it off, the intensity of her reaction to Rhys was much higher than her usual response to the latest rocker in town.

No. She sat up in the bed. *Take him. Then leave him.* As the frontman of a hot new metal band, he likely spent every waking moment crooning to groupies, releasing his pent-up vitality into their mouths and fucking them like dogs.

She had every right to get what she needed then spit him out.

A whiff of vanilla taunted her senses as Rhys drifted into the room. He walked up to her and kissed her hard. The sticky remnants of her cherry lollipop melted into the sweet JD lingering on his tongue. Her insides melted.

He pulled away and walked over to a sound board perched under the soft yellow glow of the overhead recessed lighting. A portable lava lamp set next to the makeshift stage added an orange-pink-aqua hue. He opened a small glass cabinet, produced two shot glasses and a bottle. Jack Daniel's. Of course. Was he her soul mate? What the fuck was she thinking.

He handed her one of the glasses, full to the brim. She licked the edge then shot it back in time with him.

After setting the glasses and bottle on a nightstand, he returned to the mini stage. She ran her hands through the lavish fur of the bear skin blanket. Rhys picked up a guitar, pure white, spattered in cherry red. The colorful glow from the lamp glimmered off the ivory body of the instrument as he plugged in a cable. A hum buzzed through the room, warming the already hot vibe.

Hypnotized by the crystal darkness of his eyes, his gaze held hers. "What do you want to hear?"

Immediately one band came to her mind. "Zeppelin."

Rhys smiled. Heat flushed the back of her neck.

He fingered the strings in an electric dance. The kaleidoscopic vibe wove through the room. A solo performance unfolded, just for her. The bear fur swallowed her up as she laid back against the bed. Her body writhed with every note he sang. The riff heightened to a climax. His voice followed the chords, smooth yet unrefined.

The performance ended.

Rhys placed the guitar back on a stand, turned off the sound system, and made his way to her.

Bailey's heart palpitated in rapid bursts. Butterflies flittered through her belly. She couldn't pull her eyes from his.

Braydon's face materialized in her mind. A ghost from the past with a hand on her heart. She willed the image to dissolve.

Rhys leaned over her, pushing her back against the soft fur. He slipped off her pleather pants, dropping them to the floor, then pulled her t-shirt over her head. Bra-less, her breasts ached for his touch. Next, he hooked his fingers around her black lace panties and slid them down her legs.

The room swelled with tantric heat.

From the bottle of JD from the nightstand he poured two ample shots. They downed the toxin in unison. He refilled his glass, then drizzled it down her neck and over her breasts. As he trailed the liquor over her abdomen, down her thigh, and trickled it over her throbbing sex, she trembled and clutched the fur. He set the empty shot glass on the nightstand then planted kisses over her left breast, then her right, lingering over her nipple. Sandwiched between his tongue and the bear fur, her skin blazed.

Rhys made his way down to her abdomen, pausing slightly above her sweet spot. Her entire body shuddered in anticipation. As he lapped up the JD, she purred. Her head tilted back, her skin melded with the soft fur of the blanket.

The room spun in a rainbow of color. Bailey succumbed to the pleasure, despite the warning whispering in the back of her mind that her reaction might be more than physical.

Algae Bloom

As Bailey walked along the boardwalk, an image of the woman washed ashore, bloody holes in her flesh, flashed along the shoreline. Bile curdled in her stomach as she recalled the odor steaming from the body. She took a whiff of the cheese enchilada in the bag hanging from her arm to dissolve the clinging stench. Her stomach grumbled. She was eager to stay in bed all day, sleeping off her night at 720 Beach House. Simmering in the remnants of her private after party with Rhys, the metal angel. The scent of vanilla still clung to her senses, reminding her that she'd silently slipped out of his hotel room only an hour ago.

The midnight sky twinkled under a blanket of stars, casting little diamonds over the dark water. A thunderous wave rolled in the distance. She imagined the depths of the ocean pulling the woman's body down to whatever had bitten her. The spray from the ocean caught on the slight breeze and misted over her face. She sighed. Picking up her pace, she hurried along the last few blocks.

There were too many signs that something with fangs was hovering near the surface. The images haunted Bailey, matching the memories from years ago when Braydon was pulled to his watery death. That horrifying day when she'd been accused of experiencing panic and fear-infused hallucinations. If only Braydon's body hadn't washed out to sea, taking away any proof of a fanged creature.

She forced the images from her thoughts. Amping up her pace, she concentrated on reaching the turn-off from the boardwalk that would take her home.

A fluorescent light flashed on the beach. The moon's light revealed glowing contours along the shore. The muscles in her legs clenched, rooting her to the boardwalk, bolting her to a stop. Gelatinlike mounds scattered over the beach, reminding her of a jellyfish obliterated by a strong wave and thrown ashore. She'd seen it happen many times, but this was different. A purple gleam coated the viscous globs as they shimmered under the starlight. The luminescence suddenly intensified.

She blinked hard. *I'm crazy. It's in my mind.*

Something slammed into her back, crushing her stomach against the concrete half-wall separating the boardwalk from the beach. The sound of skin scraping across pavement morphed into a loud moan.

Bailey shook her head, seeking the source of the body slam, and the moaning. The crumpled body of a teenage boy lay on the ground. He curled into a half ball and clutched at the shredded skin on his knee as blood trickled down his shin.

"Fuck me. That hurt," he yelped.

A skateboard clink-clanked across the concrete then bumped into the half wall.

Bailey steadied herself. "Are you okay?"

He opened his eyes. "Fuck. Did I run into you? I'm sorry."

"No problem."

"No way. I hit hard."

"Really. I'm okay."

His eyes widened. "What the hell? Did you see that? The light?"

"You mean that?" Bailey pointed over the half wall.

The teen stood and stumbled. "What the hell is it?"

Bailey froze, mesmerized by the purple humps. Glowing. Pulsing. Like they were breathing. Like they were alive. "I don't know."

Taco Time

Pacific Beach Fish House appeared ahead. Bailey rolled on her skates through the entrance to the year-round patio that housed the majority of the seating. Gannon sat on a bench bordering a table decorated in colorful glass chips. Bright blues, vibrant greens, and cosmic aquas formed an abstract pattern, making her think of the ocean. He didn't see her as he concentrated hard on an open notebook. She rolled over to him. The sun glinted off a section of purple glass composing the tabletop. The glowing jelly sacs scattered across the beach flashed through her mind.

She plunked down across from Gannon. "Hey."

"You're late." Gannon inspected his watch.

"What? By a minute?" She pursed her lips.

"Try ten." He concentrated on his notebook.

"Oh. Sorry. I wasted ten minutes of your life." She frowned.

"I got a paper due."

"You *always* have a paper due. All you do is obsess over every detail about some fish who lives down at the bottom of the sea, scouring a million sources and the stack of handwritten notes from the last dive you took in the Sea Otter." She threw her hands in the air. Her exhaustion was getting to her. She'd barely slept after her night on the beach with the glowing purple humps.

"It's the Sea *Lion.* No one calls a deep diving research machine an otter." He straightened his glasses and abandoned his notes. "Geez. You look terrible."

"I'm tired. I was up all night. I didn't call you here for kicks." Her frown eased as she watched concern form in his eyes.

He closed his notebook. "I'm sorry. What happened?"

"Hell of a night. I need your help. But first, I need a beer." She stood up. "Let me buy you a fresh fish taco. I bet you haven't eaten all day."

"Okay. I guess I haven't eaten since…"

"Let me guess… You popped out of bed and bolted straight to the lab, brain buzzing, ideas flying." She smirked.

"Yeah. You know me."

"What ya want?"

"I'd love a mahi-mahi. Oh, and if they have the sea bass, one of those. They're delicious. Taste like butter."

"Sounds good. And a drink?" She stood and rolled away.

"Nothing alcoholic," he hollered after her.

She ignored him, rolled across the patio and to the front door of the restaurant. The small interior housed a few tables and a massive glass case displaying a plethora of fresh fish. Bailey eyeballed the tunas, salmon, swordfish, and other daily catches. A handwritten sign plunged into the bed of ice. *Sea Bass. Good.* Gannon would be happy.

After ordering four tacos, a can of Cali Creamin', and a bottle of Green Flash IPA, she rolled away with a beer in each hand.

She set the IPA in front of Gannon on the table.

"I told you, no alcohol."

She narrowed her eyes. "It's *one* beer. And it might relax you. Just think of how the words will write themselves when you get back to the lab."

Shrugging his shoulders, he picked up the bottle and took a swig.

Bailey took a long gulp of the cream ale and reclined against the bench. "I don't know how I've stayed friends with you all these years. You're such a square."

"Well, I don't know how I've stayed friends with you. You've become such a party slut." He smirked at his bold remark.

"Yeah, well, what's a girl supposed to do? Find a clean-cut surfer boyfriend?" She stuck her tongue out.

"Now that would be a start. You might actually be happy, though. Wouldn't want that."

The comment cut her in the gut. Her shoulders clenched. There was a huge amount of truth behind it. Braydon flashed into her mind, his sun-bleached hair, tanned body, and muscles ready to take on any wave.

Gannon's hand found hers. "Hey, I'm sorry. That was too far. I'm not good at socializing." He shook his head. "They keep me locked in the lab for a reason."

"No, no. It's fine." She grabbed her beer and clicked it against his bottle. "Here's to beer and fish tacos."

"Hey, it's nice hanging out. I don't leave the lab much. And I miss seeing you. This is fun."

"It is."

"But you dragged me out of the lab for more than a friendly catch-up."

"Yeah." She recalled her late-night walk home along the boardwalk after her private party with her latest catch—Rhys. "I did. I saw something really freakin' weird last night, along Pacific Beach." Pressing her fingertips against her temples, she massaged in small circles. "You've *got* to investigate this. Dammit, I wish I had a picture. I need to know what these things are." She bit her lower lip.

"What *things?*" He appeared to be interested. Or concerned.

A waiter walked up to their table, tray in hand. "Four fish tacos. Two mahi-mahi, two sea bass."

"Thank you," Bailey said.

The waiter snatched up the number perched on the table, then walked away.

"Yes, I *love* sea bass." Gannon lunged for the taco.

Fresh fish, lightly grilled, taunted her. Purple fluorescence pulsed in her mind. "Yeah, *things.* On my way home last night, I saw the weirdest things on the beach, all along Pacific. Hell, they looked like they were all up and down the shore, in both directions."

"What?" A chunk of sea bass fell from Gannon's mouth. He swallowed, wrenching himself from the fish taco. "What are you talking about?"

"They were jellylike globs, in the sand, and were everywhere. I mean, *everywhere.*" She searched her mind, double-checking her information. "They were glowing." She explored his expression, wanting his honest reaction.

"Glowing?" His lips contorted into a weird shape.

"Yeah. Purple. Fluorescent. One second it was dark, the next, they were all illuminated. Like they had all turned on somehow, together."

"Purple?"

"Yeah."

"What time was this?"

"Uh, I dunno. Late."

"Right after a show?" He narrowed his eyes, then lunged in for another bite of sea bass.

"No. I, uh, went out after."

"Another private after party? Just you and some poor rocker sucker."

"Fine. I went home with the lead singer. Why does it matter what time it was, anyway?"

"Just getting a feel for where you were at in your evening."

Her mind clicked. She glared at him. "Oh, you think I was drunk. Or high. You think I imagined it." She grabbed his arm. "Listen, I know what I saw. And I wasn't the only one who saw it. I swear. Some teenager knocked the wind out of me on his skateboard. The glowing purple beach caught his attention." She took a deep breath.

"Was anyone notified?"

"I ran up to the guard station. No one was there. I radioed it in." She sighed. "By the time the guard got there, the glowing had stopped." She threw her hands in the air. "He inspected the things. I followed along. They were like sacs of jelly, gooey, gross."

Gannon continued to gorge on his taco, disbelief in his eyes.

"Listen, Gannon, it happened. I need to know what the hell these things were. Something fucked up is happening in the ocean. What if it has something to do with whatever killed that woman?"

Gannon set down the taco. "All right. I believe you. Purple glowing sand humps." He frowned. "It is suspicious—the iridescent glow. Didn't you say you saw the same thing when you were rescuing that boy? A glow? Right before you got bitten?"

"Yeah." She swallowed. "And…"

"What?" He pushed his glasses up the bridge of his nose. "It's *me*. I told you. I believe you. Now spit it out."

"I *did* see the glow when I swam out to that boy the other day. I also saw it when Braydon died." She swallowed again. "You know my version. You know what I saw. The bite marks. The stench. Do you remember me telling you about a purple light under the surface?"

Gannon pushed his plate away and clenched his jaw. "I do remember. You did say that." He placed his hand on her shoulder. "And when the Sea Lion got bit. Remember, I told you…they saw a purple light."

"So, what do you think?"

"Chemosynthesis."

"What?"

"Above the surface, the sun provides energy to living beings. Photosynthesis."

"We thrive off the heat from the sun."

"Deep enough, there is no sunlight. It can't possibly pierce that far down. It's pitch black. Thus, chemosynthesis. It's a process of generating energy, in the darkest depths, without the sun. The marine life that far down flourishes from it."

"Just like the bikini-clad beachgoers thrive off the sun."

"Precisely. There are fish that are luminescent. Most of them are deep dwellers. The light primarily serves to lure prey or confuse predators. In some cases, it can be a navigation system." He guzzled his beer. "Purple?"

"Yeah, purple."

"The viperfish has three photophores. Kind of blueish purple. Also has needle-like teeth. Could explain the purple glow and the bite marks. Does live in the Northeast Pacific. But…only comes up during the day, and only to about fifteen hundred meters under."

"Is there anything glowing that lives near the surface?"

"Pinecone fish—all along the Eastern Pacific Ocean. Hangs out in coral reefs and caves. But they're orange by day and blue-green by night."

"So we have shallow *or* purple. Not both." Bailey stared at the rainbow-colored glass tabletop.

"These are two examples that pop to mind. There are at least fifteen hundred bioluminescent species of fish in the ocean. That we know of. I'd need some time to dig into this. And it doesn't explain glowing sacs all over the beach. The only incandescent things that I can think of that wash ashore are algae blooms, when disturbed by dolphins or waves. The bright color can be dazzling."

"I did see flashes of light. I swear." She took a long pull from her beer. "I know. It's far-fetched. I get it, I sound crazy.

But I know what I saw. The teenager saw it too." She chugged the rest of her cream ale and slapped the can on the table.

Gannon swallowed the last bit of sea bass taco. "You said they stopped glowing?"

"Yeah."

"They were like sacs of jelly?" He wiped his hands with a thin paper napkin.

"When the lifeguard arrived, I followed him. We got up close. They were just wet, gooey clumps. He said it was nothing. I suspect he was annoyed I called. He didn't believe me that they were glowing. The teenager had split by then." She fidgeted with the empty beer can.

"You know the lifeguard?"

"John. He's kind of a dick." She placed the beer can on the table and stared at the purple glass. "He dismissed it. That was the end of it."

"I believe you. I've been swamped and totally abandoned my dead-end search for a fish with fangs, but I need to find time to help you. We have a set of weird clues here. We need to find out if your purple glowing jelly sacs have anything to do with an iridescent fish with fangs."

Her shoulders relaxed. "How do we do that?"

"Well, I'm gonna start by finishing this taco." He slid the mahi-mahi taco across the table. "Then we'll make a stop at Pacific Beach. Maybe we'll get lucky and the sacs haven't all washed away. Then I'll go back to the lab and start digging through the database for purple glowing things and fish with fangs."

"What about your paper?"

"The sea creatures aren't going anywhere." He smiled as he took a big bite of fresh fish.

Body on the Rocks

A group of harbor seals swam up to the shore, barking at each other. They reached the shoreline and shimmied over the sand like giant worms, looking for the perfect spot. Rolling over in the sand, they turned onto their backs, sunning their bellies. Half a dozen children scattered on the beach, giggling in delight.

A thunderous wave crashed against the far side of the sea wall, sending a spray over the railing and trickles of water down the side facing the beach. The tide was extra high today. Bailey contemplated keeping the sea wall closed off for an additional hour. As soon as she opened the rope across the entranceway at the top of the stairwell, the children would surely run over, seeking a prime position to view the harbor seals.

Bailey didn't want an accident on her watch. She'd been looking forward to an easy shift. Unfortunately, the La Jolla station was short-staffed, and she'd been sent up the shore.

Despite her attempts, she'd been unable to replenish her energy on her day off. She couldn't sleep after seeing the purple glowing things on the beach. And she couldn't believe that the dickhead lifeguard had brushed off her story.

After watching Gannon devour the mahi-mahi tacos, they scoured Pacific Beach. Nothing resembling a sac of jelly could be found. Every remnant of a glowing, purple hump was gone. He'd dropped her off and made his way back to Scripps, insisting he'd dig up some information while she tried to get some sleep. Instead, her mind buzzed with a million images and thoughts. The past few days had left her in a manic state.

The experience of seeing the dead woman on the beach, the terrifying rescue of the boy across the wake, and the strange purple jelly-like things on her walk home after the show had caused the memories of Braydon that she'd stifled to resurface in a flood. To top it off, the intensity of her reaction to Rhys left her reeling with emotions she hadn't experienced since the last time Braydon touched her.

Up to this point, she'd maintained control, keeping her nights with rock singers nothing more than a physical experience, and none of them had objected. With Rhys, it had been different.

Rhys had his own agenda, and every part of her had succumbed despite the turmoil that had washed through her. He was like a drug. Not just a potent joint. Not like all the other rockers she'd taken for a spin, then left high and dry when finished. No. She couldn't just take one, long drag of Rhys then forget about him. All she could think about was his vanilla scent, his eyes searching her, and his hands strumming his guitar at the private show he gave her, then running all over her body.

That guitar. The custom paint job had captivated her. Pure white spattered in cherry red. He'd said it was a JS32Q body with a mid-nineties performance neck. She couldn't believe she'd remembered the details. Every word he'd spoken to her since she'd met him stuck vividly in her mind.

A screech snapped her from her reverie.

Two kids ran across the sand, yelling out, declaring that the seals were so cute, so much fun. Bailey watched them play. It was one of her favorite spots, but she didn't get up to La Jolla often. Her roller skates weren't adequate to get her up the coast this far. And the boardwalk ended on the edge of Pacific Beach.

This spot was a gem. The sea wall closed off the savage ocean, to create a circular pool of calmer water. It was a safe spot for kids to swim. The harbor seals found refuge from the dangers in the depths of the ocean and came in to rest and sun themselves on the shore.

A high-pitched scream snatched Bailey's attention.

A young girl cried, "Mommy! He's hurt." She pointed at a small seal, rolling around in the sand, blotches of red seeping from his side.

What the hell? Bailey bolted down the stairs, onto the beach, and ran over to the girl and the wounded seal.

A woman ran up beside her, yelling, "Lisa, get away from it." The woman grabbed the girl by the arm and pulled her away.

Other children had gathered, crowding the scene, staring and pointing at the bloody seal.

Bailey crouched down and inspected the seal's body. She found a set of three holes in the side of the seal's slippery flesh. Blood poured from the wells, soaking the sand.

Her breath quickened. These were the same bite marks she'd seen far too much of lately. On the woman who'd washed ashore in Mission Beach. On her own leg after breaking over the wake and saving the drowning boy in Pacific Beach. On Braydon's leg before his body got pulled away from her clutches by a massive wave. And now, on this small seal barking and roiling in pain. What the hell was going on?

The seal wriggled against the rocks. A larger seal sidled over, rearing its head and barking at Bailey.

She backed off.

Bailey shooed the children over to the staircase then climbed the stairs after them and strode over to the lifeguard truck parked right beside the walkway. She grabbed a rope, tied off the entranceway to the stairwell, and walked back to the truck to radio for assistance.

Another screech pierced the air, stopping Bailey in her tracks. A shrill voice cried, "Oh my God."

Bailey sprinted to the walkway, facing the beach. A woman stood, towering over the railing, looking at the beach below. She pointed over to the sea wall on the other side of the beach. At the very tip of the wall, at the end of its circular shape, a body bobbed, lulling with the motion of the water, bumping against the rocks.

What fresh hell is this? Bailey's mind buzzed. She already knew the answer. She had no doubt the body would have three holes somewhere. Deep wells in the flesh. Caverns of blood.

Several women gathered the children, herding them away from the walkway. At least Bailey wouldn't have to deal with crowd control. She thanked her lucky stars it wasn't a weekend, when the crowds packed in tight, locals mixing with tourists to get a look at the cute little seals.

Bailey hurried to the truck, hoisted herself up into the back bed, slipped off her flip-flops, and pulled on a pair of rubber boots with strong grips. The sea wall would be slick. The last thing she wanted was to plummet into the water next to a dead body.

After pulling a sweater on, she made her way to the stairway leading up to the sea wall. With cautious steps, she tested each boot placement before ascending the next stair.

Reaching the entrance, she unlatched the rope, stepped onto the sea wall, then relatched the rope.

A stitch clawed at her gut. Why did she have to see another corpse? It seemed lately death popped up whenever she was near the shore. It was as if the sea monster sinking its teeth into flesh was leaving a trail of bodies specifically for her.

I sound ridiculous.

Moving along the sea wall, her boots gripped the hazardous concrete as she held the railing and walked to the end. She swallowed, took a deep breath, then scoured the water.

Small waves lapped against the body of a young man, pushing it into the wall. A shiny, black wetsuit hung in shreds. Red scrapes ran down the sides of his face, like rug burns. The water splashed and the body bobbed. His face scraped against the rough sea wall. *Splash. Bump. Scrape. Splash. Bump. Scrape.* Bailey willed the sound to stop, but it persisted.

A stench rose up from the water below in a sudden wave—the smell of death and decay. No, more than that. The smell of fresh rot seeping with gases. The same odor she'd detected when the woman washed ashore on Mission Beach, only days before.

She leaned over as far as she could, inspecting the open wounds running down the exposed arms and legs. Punctures ripped through the remaining pieces of wetsuit into the flesh. Multiple sets of three bite marks riddled his legs and arms: one on each thigh, one on the right shin, one on the left shoulder, one on the side of his face, and another in the side of his head, pink mush spilling out of the holes.

Bailey gagged. Globs of the fresh avocado she'd eaten that morning came back up. Disgusted, she'd seen *and* smelled enough.

Bailey made her way back along the sea wall, clinging to the railing, but the bloody caverns wedged in her mind. In a flash, she was back to that day, on the other side of the surf with Braydon. Exposed in the open water, the ocean surrounding them in all directions. Rocking up and down in an easy flow, laying on their surfboards. Waiting for the next big wave. Far from the wake, beyond the pier that stretched out from Ocean Beach, reaching into the deep water.

Her foot slipped on a glob of algae. She grabbed the railing and steadied herself then continued along the sea wall, on her mission back to the truck to radio for help.

The bite marks stuck in her mind. Those same bite marks that riddled Braydon's flesh as she held his convulsing body in her arms. Bailey could still feel the acid in her stomach curdling, the screams of help sticking in her throat, and her limbs freezing as she stared in helpless awe, watching him succumb to his horrific end.

One minute, he was there, and the next he was gone, torn from her grip by a torrential wave. When the water had calmed, he was nowhere in sight, and a stench had risen from the water. A smell of rot and decay, like nothing Bailey had ever experienced in her life. The same stench she walked away from only days before on Mission Beach. The same smell emanating now from the water at the tip of the sea wall.

Bailey stepped from the last stair, leaving the sea wall and reaching the walkway along the beach. She sprinted to the truck, then yanked the passenger door open, hoisted herself up onto the seat, and laid her head back against the headrest.

Why was this happening? What was she supposed to do? The bite marks, the stench, the look on the dead man's face— there was no denying the fresh images of death flashing through her mind now matched those hiding in the crevices of her memories. Back then, no one had believed her. They said she was temporarily insane, traumatized by the accident, in shock from watching her best friend, her lover, die.

What would happen now?

There was proof. This was the second body with the same marks to wash ashore in a matter of days. The ones throbbing in pain in her own thigh added a third set of matching blueprints. There was also the seal, bleeding out on the beach below. Then why did doubt cloud her mind, threatening to deem her crazy again?

Bailey opened her eyes, grabbed the radio, and pushed the button. "La Jolla Station calling main base." She released the button. White noise crackled. A sigh of defeat escaped her lips.

"This is main base."

Relief washed over her. Bailey pushed the button again. Her weak voice cracked, "Request assistance. Seal beach. Seal down. Man down."

"Come again?"

"There's a dead body floating with the seals," she yelled

into the radio, released the button, then laid her head back against the seat and swallowed hard.

More Rhys

Bailey blazed along the empty boardwalk on her roller skates in an attempt to obliterate the images of the corpses invading her mind. An orange-pink hue glowed over the horizon, stretching across the ocean. White boards and black-suited surfers coasted along the crest of a huge wave, rolling to the shore. A cluster of seagulls stood at the edge of the water, their squeals competing with the sound of the surf.

After tossing around in her crumpled sheets for hours, she gave up. She couldn't sleep and needed to clear her head. Every time she had closed her eyes and willed sleep to come, the dead faces had materialized, clear and gruesome. The woman, her black hair sticking to her pale face in matted clumps. The red caverns plunging into her arms and legs. Sea bugs crawled over her, into her tangled hair, her eye sockets, and in and out of the bloody holes that had killed her. The young diver, his suit ripped to shreds, his face scraping against the sea wall, the holes in his head oozing with bloody pink brain mush.

That stench. The odor of all odors that still remained in the back of her throat despite the number of shots of Jack Daniel's she threw back. Nothing would get rid of the images or the smell.

She reached the cul-de-sac near 720. Clusters of tattered people huddled along a patch of grass, finding refuge in one of the few places along the boardwalk that the authorities let them rest. Easing to a slow roll, she contemplated what to do. Turn around and skate back to her apartment? Then what. Sleep was impossible. It was even too early to call Gannon, and she didn't want to interrupt what little rest he got. The whole day stretched out in front of her like a gaping hole. She was off duty, again—protocol after finding a dead body scraping against the sea wall. But she'd rather be on shift. Then at least she'd have something to focus on. And she could watch the wake for predators.

"Bailey," a voice broke her reverie.

She confronted the source and froze. Her heart seized. She wished for a cavern to open and swallow her.

Rhys. The first rocker to turn her plans to devour and split into an all-night cosmic experience of sweet Jack Daniel's, a private Zeppelin show, and an electric rush through her entire body. *Dammit.* Why did she have to deal with this right now?

"Bailey." He ran up to her, his boots thudding against the pavement.

The aroma of dark roast wafted from a tray of large paper cups, held secure by a cardboard to-go cup holder perched in his hand.

"Man, am I happy to see you." He ran his metal-ring-adorned hand through his hair, hooking a long strand behind his ear. A lock broke free, dancing over one of his dark eyes.

She shook off the shock seizing her body. "Oh yeah?" She either imagined that she'd rolled her eyes, or she really had. Feeling unsure, she hoped it was the former.

"Yeah. We're headed out of town. Sunrise is spectacular here. I should get away from the big city more often." He moved closer to her. Vanilla scent overtook the strong coffee.

She breathed in without meaning to. *Double dammit.* "Safe travels then." She rolled in a circle, facing the boardwalk.

He touched her arm with his free hand. "Bailey. Wait."

The sunrise glowed a pink-orange. He was right. It *was* beautiful. A dolphin blasted from the wave, body arched, dancing alongside a surfer catching the wave. The dolphins out there had loved Braydon. They had swum with him every morning.

Rhys's voice dissolved the image, forcing her attention. "I called. A million times." His cheeks flushed.

The piece of paper, torn from a notebook beside the bed, flashed through her mind. Why had she left her number?

He examined his feet, then her. "I was really hoping we could spend more time together, before the band moves on."

"Oh yeah?" She turned and faced him, eye to eye. "Why? Get your kicks before the next town?"

"It's not like that." Confusion riddled his expression. He shook his head. His hair floated in the slight morning breeze. "I believed we connected."

"Oh, we connected. You got your connection, multiple times over." Her breakfast avocado curdled in her stomach. What was she doing? "Don't worry. You'll find another groupie for your private after-show at the next town." *Bailey, stop it.* "I'm sure she'll suck you off just fine. Meet all your needs." *Bailey, you're an asshole.* She swallowed against the self-loathing lurking in her throat.

Rhys blinked. "Well, I'm sorry you think that's all it was." His eyes searched hers.

Passionate tremors ran through her. She hadn't felt like this since…Braydon.

Rhys drove home his point. "I didn't." He turned, coffee in hand, and headed down the street.

Bailey rocked back and forth on the wheels of her skates. The pain-rage-fear concoction building inside muted her voice. Her body numbed as she watched Rhys walk out of her life.

Surf

The sleek blue board cut through the water, heading straight for the oncoming wake. Bailey swallowed back the ball of fear in her throat as she faced the massive watery mound head-on. Amping her paddling up to a manic row, she forced her way into the wave. Encased in a water house, white-aqua swirls obscuring her vision, she burst through the other side.

Across the wake, she bobbed on the calm water, the sun warming her skin and creating dancing sparkles across the glassy surface. A sense of peace warmed her to the core. Everything stopped. Frozen in a moment in time, she gazed far into the distance.

How long had it been since she'd made it across the surf? Not counting the other day, of course. The other day, she'd been forced to venture out beyond the safe zone to save a drowning boy. With no time to think, she'd acted. The freak-out came after.

The boy was fine. His emotional scars would heal. The constant throbbing in her leg was a reminder that she was the only one who had suffered any physical injuries. The damage was done—years ago, when she lost Braydon. And now, when the stinky, glowing purple fish had bit her.

After running into Rhys, she realized she was tired of hiding from the past, and sick of being afraid. She was done with the brick of fear sitting in the pit of her gut. As she bobbed, lulling with the flow of the water, she decided it was time to be free.

The liquid courage she'd brought with her in her lucky flask, secured in her wetsuit pocket, wasn't even necessary.

Made of stainless steel molded into a custom design, it was her favorite piece of band swag. With the logo, Steeletto, engraved into a separate piece of metal that swung out, the dramatic points of the *S* and each *T* protruded like blades.

The next wave loomed ahead, reeling over her. She braced herself and steadied her body against the smooth, long board. Stretching out her leg, the line went taut and the strap around her ankle tugged. *Secured?* Yes. *Ready?* No. *Now or never.* She gritted her teeth and told herself not to back down.

The next wave rolled in. She pressed hard against her shiny blue board streaked in silver. The wave intensified, its massive, white body swelling and careening toward her. The muscles in her arms and legs rippled as she paddled.

At the ideal moment, she popped her body up and latched her feet to her board. She flew up with the wave, reached the peak, and soared over the ocean surface. The sea sprayed her face, her hair. Riding the momentum, she coasted. The world around her diminished to nothing but an open ocean. The brick in the bottom of her stomach vanished. The ball of turmoil spinning inside of her flashed away as if it had never existed. She breathed in deep, closed her eyes, and became one with the wave. Every neuron in her brain buzzed, every nerve ending sparked.

Wham.

Something hard hit the side of her board. She flew through the air, then plunged into the ocean. A massive mouth of a wave crashed down, eating her up like a tiny fish. The watery vortex pulled her down. Bailey swam like mad, pushing the water down in wild strokes, launching herself up to the sun breaking through the surface above. The wave subsided. The swirling undercurrent eased. Her head popped up, like a seal coming up for life-giving breath. Her board joined a second later, popping up out of the water, then floating beside her.

Something slipped along her leg. She jerked. Her mind seized. She scanned the water, seeking the source of whatever had knocked her off her board. The water was like glass, rhythmic ripples dotting the smooth sheet.

Was she imagining things? *No.* Something had pounded into the side of her board. She was sure of it.

The slippery thing again wrapped around her ankle and slithered up her leg. Her jaw clenched. She pulled her leg out of the water. A long strand of gooey algae coiled her shin.

She shook her head. *Stupid. Just algae.*

Bailey went to work removing the slimy plant. She pulled the last bit away and threw it into the water.

A splash, followed by a ripple, shattered the peaceful quiet. Bailey watched and waited. Whatever it was might resurface. Another splash. Another ripple. She paddled toward it. A purple fluorescence flickered a few feet away. A smooth body flipped out of the water then resubmerged. A fin poked through the water then thrust ahead, leaving a wake as it sliced a path moving away from her. The fish dove, disappearing underneath. Luminescence clung to the ripples.

A series of images rushed her mind… The beach covered in glowing jelly sacs. The purple flash when she saved the drowning boy. The day she watched something eat Braydon alive, a purple shimmer emanating from the aqua as he plunged to his watery death.

She slid over to her board, pressing her stomach against the warm fiberglass. Rotating her arms, she guided her board over the water. She gained speed. Another splash ahead. Another ripple followed by a purple glow. Pulling at the water faster with her hands, salty droplets poured down her face and she breathed hard from the exertion. Desperate to hunt down the source of the luminescence, she refused to give up.

A bulbous body covered in scales popped out of the water, racing away, leaving a rippling wake. Its unnatural hue hypnotized her. Determined to see for herself what had killed the young woman on Mission Beach and what had pierced its teeth into the head of the diver in La Jolla, leaving his brain to ooze out the holes, she chased the fish. It might be her only chance to find out what had killed Braydon.

The creature halted and the fin circled as it turned. She gained on the mystery fish as it hovered ahead. Suddenly, it darted, coming straight at her with tremendous speed.

She searched around in a panic. *Her flask.* She unzipped the pocket in her wetsuit, grabbed the flask in a white-knuckle grip, and spun the sharpened points of the band logo out into a makeshift, multi-bladed knife.

The purple glow rippled over the surface, obscuring the shape of the creature charging her. Bailey frantically stroked, thrusting her board forward.

The creature, closing in on her, gained speed. Her board continued to slice through the water as she aimed directly at the fin.

In a head-on collision, her board smashed into the creature. The force shot the board upward, flinging Bailey through the air. The safety line pulled tight, yanking her back to the water. Bailey hit the ocean with a loud splash and plummeted straight down, her hand clutching her flask. Pain sliced her ankle as blood gushed, turning the water murky. A large shadow inched by, the form of the creature obscured.

The water diluted the blood, exposing the mystery fish. The fin turned again.

A scaly, spheric body lunged for her. She inspected the dark water, trying to see the creature in its entirety. A vein-riddled tentacle of flesh protruded from the top of the creature, reaching for her. Bright light emitted a strobe-like pattern from a bulb, held by the tip of the tentacle. Radiance lit up the gloomy underwater world in a brilliant flare. She stifled a scream.

Three long glassy fangs reached for her.

She released a mess of bubbles and forced her arm through the heavy water, thrusting the flask at the scaly creature.

The sharp steel plunged into the glowing purple flesh. A black burst clouded the water. An inky ooze followed, painting the aqua in a gruesome display.

The fangs sank into her shoulder as fresh blood burst over them. The long teeth slid out of her flesh, leaving deep wells. More blood followed. Black sea creature blood mixed with her own scarlet stream, painting the pristine aqua of the ocean in horrid streaks.

A long blue, curved body sped by in a flash. The watery world blurred around her. A swirl of white-aqua-red-black engulfed her as her body went limp and she plunged down into the dark. She sank into the depths, her ankle pulling the safety line with her until the line went taut and the board floating above pulled back. Her body halted as the line pulled tighter until it snapped. Bailey descended, into the oblivion of the deep ocean.

Beached

A cocktail of saltwater, stomach acid, and regurgitated avocado gushed from her mouth. A foul aftertaste soured the back of Bailey's throat. She coughed and sputtered, rolling onto her side, staring down at her partially digested breakfast caking the sand.

What the hell happened?

Her head throbbed. Hot pain sliced her shoulder and her shin. Blood oozed from both wounds.

Bailey contorted her neck, head throbbing harder, and inspected her shoulder. Three matching red holes stared back at her, fresh blood seeping from them and down her arm.

After all this time she'd finally swam past the wake and crested a wave. Everything was perfect until the purple glow and scaly fish intruded upon her peaceful moment. Finally, she'd gotten a real glimpse of the creature. The veiny bulb and glassy fangs were terrifying.

Why had she gotten away? *The flask.*

She'd cut that fucking fish. But it had bitten her.

Where was she? Where was her board?

A watery voice echoed through the space around her. Was she still under the water?

The pile of regurgitated breakfast, blood, and salty water caught her gaze. No. She was on the beach. But how?

The voice wove through her ears. She squinted into the bright sun. A fuzzy face hung over her, moving through the blinding rays. The brightness eased and the face became clear.

Craig? Did he pull her from the water?

"Bailey." His clear voice pierced her ears. "Can you hear me?"

She nodded. Clumps of her hair, coated in scarlet, stuck to her cheek. She raised her arm and pulled the hair behind her ear. Blood seeped over her fingers.

"She's coming to," Craig's watery voice shook. "Get the stretcher. Now." He smiled at her. "Bailey, lay back down and relax." He put his hand on her good shoulder.

Nodding again, she let him ease her back onto the sand. Her heavy head throbbed. A morsel of clarity returned to her thoughts. She knew she should do what he asked of her. The hardest thing was a half-drowned surfer who disregarded the instructions of the lifeguard who had pulled their sorry ass out of the ocean.

She lay still as her adventure replayed in her mind. Cresting the wave, and finding peace with the ocean, after all this time.

The purple glow beneath the surface followed by the fin racing at her causing a head-on collision. It had launched her into the air, and she'd sunk into the ocean. The steel points of her flask had cut into that damn fish. She knew she'd wounded it. How bad? It bit her, twice. The darkness pulling her down in the water clouded her logic.

The sky spun. Bailey's stomach swirled. She went limp against the sand as the world faded out.

Mutation

Bailey screamed as fangs, glassy and sharp, reached for her. Bolting upright, her eyes flung open, and her nostrils stung with sterilization. Purple lights oscillated through her brain and the back of her head hammered. The smell of death and rot suffocated her. The images refused to subside.

White walls enclosed her in a stuffy room. The nurse had told her to rest. How could she when the images invaded her every thought? When that fucking fish was still out there? How many more innocent swimmers would it feast on? The ball of instinct in her gut clenched harder. Something was lurking in the depths and it *was* the same fucking fish that bit Braydon, pierced his flesh, drained the life from him, and caused his plunge into the ocean. No one had believed her. Everyone had deemed her insane, overtaken by panic and fear-infused hallucinations.

His body had somehow washed out into the depths of the ocean, forever lost. No body. No bite marks. No proof.

The door swung open, snapping her from her downward spiral. Gannon appeared, closing the door behind him. His tousled hair and crooked glasses made Bailey smile despite the throbbing pain in her head, the hot knives slicing through her leg and her shoulder, and the sterile stench violating her senses.

"Bailey, are you okay?"

She smirked. "I've seen better days. But yeah, I'm fine."

He walked up to her. "You were lucky."

"I guess. Don't think that fucking fish is dead."

"They didn't find it."

"It's still out there?" Her temples throbbed as heat flushed her cheeks.

"You need to relax." He pressed a hand against her shoulder, guiding her back against the scratchy pillow.

"Can't. It's so stiff and sterile in here. All I can think about is that purple beast and its fangs." Her head whirled.

"You shouldn't have been out there." Gannon produced an ample handful of lollipops from his pocket. He piled them onto the plastic table beside her bed.

"Oh. My. God. You are an angel." She grabbed a bright red one, unwrapped it, and slid it into her mouth. She rested her head against the pillow and savored the sweet treat. "Oh yeah, baby."

Gannon giggled. "Figured you'd be missing your addictions in here." He put his hand into his other pocket and pulled out a Walkman, a set of earphones attached.

"What? Jesus. You are Jesus, aren't you?"

He set the Walkman on the table and the headphones on top. He produced a cassette case and set it next to the mini sound system.

Bailey inspected the case and saw Angels of Death written in blazing yellow lettering down the front. Her insides churned. "How'd you get that?"

"Stopped by 720. Your friend, Johnny, hooked me up. Figured he knew what bands you were into lately. Said you really enjoyed this show…Angels of Death."

Rhys's voice resonated through her ears as quivers ran down her arms and legs. "Yeah. It was a good show." She ran her fingers over the cassette case. "Thanks, Gannon, really."

"Anything for you. You know, you really shouldn't have been out there. I mean, if it wasn't for that lifeguard…"

"Craig. Right." She could still feel the black depths of the water closing in on her. "I was falling…to the bottom."

"You were knocked out cold, detached from your board. Craig swam out to you. He saved you from drowning."

"The last thing I remember is those fangs biting into me." She looked vacantly across the room. "And black ocean closing in." She sat straight up. "Gannon, it came *at* me. I mean, it was swimming away, fast. It stopped and then it turned and attacked. And it bit me. I sliced into it, I know it, with my flask." The thin hospital gown stuck to her moist skin.

"Flask?" He raised an eyebrow.

"It has a stainless-steel band emblem on it that slides out, and the letters are pointy, like little blades."

"Good time to be a rock fan." He chuckled briefly, then contemplation contorted his face. "Fish don't usually come at a human like that. If it was swimming away, why would it turn around?"

"I know. I felt…hunted."

"You didn't answer my question. Why were you out there? What were you thinking?" He gave her a stern look, like a parent scolding a child.

She whipped her head around, staring him down. She licked her dry lips. "I'm just so fucking tired of being scared of what's out there in the ocean I've loved my whole life." Her bottom lip trembled, cherry sugar sticking to it. A tear slid from the corner of her eye. "I'm so sick of being the stupid lifeguard who's afraid to go over the wake."

Gannon reached his hand over to her face, wiping away the tear with his thumb, cradling her cheek in his palm. "Hey, you're not stupid. And you're the bravest person I know."

She smiled. "Thanks."

"You have some massive balls going out there alone. Two corpses washed ashore. In between which you had your own encounter when you saved that kid. You knew something was out there."

She pulled the lollipop from her mouth with a pop. Tremors shook her red, sticky lips. "Yeah. I did. I knew it the day Braydon died." She sighed. "I just wanted to ride a wave again. To relive it. I didn't care what was out there." She swallowed, plunged the lollipop back in her mouth and rolled it around, the cherry sugar coating her tongue.

Gannon sat next to her on the bed. "So, what did you see?"

"Same things. Purple iridescent glow. Fangs. But this time, I saw more of it. The teeth were like glass. And Gannon, it has this eyeball." She pursed her lips, retrieving the image from her fuzzy mind.

Gannon sat up. "An eyeball?"

"Well, it was *like* an eyeball, but it was glowing, and it kept changing color. It was bulbous with veins slithering all over it. It was attached to this big tentacle, reaching out of its forehead." She paused, narrowing her eyes.

"Wow." Gannon shook his head.

"What?"

"This aligns with my totally wacked-out ideas."

"What are you talking about?"

"There is *nothing* in any recorded database that I have access to, or in any article I have ever read, that is a match for your glowing monster with three fangs."

"So, what? This leads us nowhere." Bailey's head pounded. Her ears rang.

"Oh, it's out there. It's just not recorded. *Yet.*" Gannon's eyes danced with excitement.

Bailey's brain buzzed. "You believe me? What I saw, it *exists?*"

"Yes, but it wasn't an eyeball. It was a light. Fish with luminescent globes attached to their heads live *thousands* of meters below. Essentially, along the ocean floor."

She ran her hands through her tangled hair. "Then how the fuck did it get up to the surface?"

"Look at this." He sat up and pulled a stack of papers from his shoulder bag. He laid them out across the sheets. Several images of massive, grotesque-looking fish formed a distorted collage of an underwater horror show.

Bailey perused the photos. She stared at the deep-sea freak show unraveling before her eyes. "What in the living hell are these?"

"Examples." Gannon produced a page displaying a massive, bulbous sea creature. A tentacle protruded from its head holding a vein-riddled sphere. The body of the fish was a sickly brown, while bright color tinted the disturbing ball that looked like an eye. Four large fangs sprang from its mouth, two on top and two on the bottom. More teeth, smaller, but razor sharp, ran all along its slippery lips.

"Anglerfish." Gannon sounded giddy. "Most famous of the bioluminescent fish. The angling structure evolved from the spines of the fish's dorsal fin. The end, your eyeball, is inhabited by large numbers of bioluminescent bacteria. This is how they emit light, usually blue. Small fish think it's a tasty treat and get lured right into the mouth."

Bailey slid the photo closer to her. Her brain swelled with heat, like it was on fire. She wasn't crazy. "Like I said, these light bulbed fish, they live deep. The anglerfish is a bit of an exception. They *tend* to live at least eight hundred meters below. They *can* come up, but it doesn't happen often or for extended periods."

"So, this *thing* could emerge." Bailey took a deep breath.

"Yes. But not for long."

"But it has *four* large fangs, not three." Bailey stared at the sharp, shiny teeth. She could feel them reaching for her flesh, making her its next meal. She shivered and licked her parched lips.

"Precisely. I'm not saying that this is the exact species that attacked you. There are hundreds of species of anglerfish and over fifteen hundred types of bioluminescent creatures. The anglerfish simply demonstrates the traits you witnessed." Gannon exhibited another page. This one displayed a long, black creature that looked like a cross between a fish and an eel. It had two large glassy fangs that grew out of the flesh of its lower lip and slid into its upper lip. "Dragonfish. Another example. They either have a lure or an organ under their eye that emits red light, a wavelength that is hard for their prey to see. They hunt rather than entice their prey. Its teeth are made of nanoscale-sized crystal particles, stronger than the teeth of piranhas or sharks. Explains how it could bite into steel and why you said they looked like glass, as well as the hunting-like behavior. My theory is that your sea creature is some kind of a mutation."

"Mutation?" Bailey's eyes blinked rapidly. "Sounds like some weird science fiction."

"Hear me out." Gannon's eyes widened. "These fish are examples to prove the existence of some of the traits that you saw. I can't find anything that emits purple light or that has three fangs. Mutation in fish species *do* happen. They can be genetic or caused by environmental changes. I've found examples of extra fins, but not teeth. I *think* your fish might have undergone multiple mutations, but to have all the traits that you've witnessed, I suspect there is more at play here." He slid a magazine, *Popular Science* on the glossy front, from his shoulder bag, flipped through it, and spread it open in front of her. "Cross-fertilization. An actual, recorded instance of one fish accidentally fertilizing the eggs of another fish. The sacs are laid in forests of algae. They look similar. If high levels of chemicals are present, it can skew the ability of the fish to pick up on the scent of their sac. The fish fertilizes the wrong eggs. A new fish, a mutation, is born." Gannon smiled at his solution to a technically infused marine life puzzle.

Bailey giggled. "So, you're suggesting what, a cross-species fish fuck?"

He laughed. "What dosage of painkiller do they have you on?"

"Not enough." She pouted.

Gannon slid the photos of the anglerfish and the dragonfish over the magazine. "What if a deep-sea species mutated, deep down. We *might* get a bioluminescent creature with a trio of strong, glassy teeth. But how is it thriving higher up for extended amounts of time? The male anglerfish conducts sexual parasitism, biting onto and attaching itself to the female."

"Disgusting," Bailey interjected.

"The deep sea is wild," Gannon straightened his glasses. "The point is, they eventually detach, the male is out of the picture, and the female lays a long, gelatinous string of eggs that floats through the ocean. What if the eggs drifted upwards and were cross-fertilized by a species dwelling closer to the surface? It's just a possibility. Something happened to enable your fish to survive longer in shallow water. It would also explain the glowing things you saw on the beach."

"It would?" That night seemed implausible.

"Egg sacs do look like jelly. They could have washed ashore. Bioluminescent bacteria from our mutated deep dweller could have migrated with the eggs."

Bailey sat back against the pillow. Her shoulders relaxed. "I'm *not* insane."

"No, you're not."

Gannon took her hand in his. "I'm not saying we know what species of fish were involved. There are many in the ocean that we likely don't even know about. I'm not even saying that we know exactly how your fish got the way it is. But I *think* something mutated and surfaced."

He reached over, and grabbed a lollipop with a blue wrapper and unwrapped it.

"Careful," she said. "Those ones are sour."

He shrugged. "I like sour."

"You would." She poked him in the ribs.

"Hey." He popped the bright blue bulb into his mouth, took a suck, and puckered up his lips.

"See, I told you."

He pulled the lollipop from his mouth. "It's good."

Gannon sat up, gathered the photos and the article, and refolded them into a neat stack.

"Now what?" she asked. "Who else knows about your ideas? Is anyone doing anything about this? Are the police taking action?"

"I've told my superiors. They all think I'm nuts. Claim the cross-fertilization article was a one-off and lacked substantial proof. But they've closed Mission Beach."

She clutched the sheets. "What about La Jolla? And what good will that do, anyway? Is anyone actually trying to stop this thing? There's lots to feast on out there. Pacific Beach. Ocean Beach." Bailey imagined glassy fangs sinking into fresh surfer flesh, wreaking havoc on the popular spot.

"Nope." Gannon sucked hard on the blue lollipop, then slid it from his mouth with a pop. "The only proof we have are the bite marks on the bodies. Nobody that has actually *seen* the fish is still alive. Except for you, but…"

"They'll say I'm having more hallucinations."

He nodded. "They're waiting for it to leave, then they'll reopen the beach."

"We have to find it."

"Right." Gannon rolled his eyes, stood, and shoved the photos into his bag.

Bailey grabbed his arm. "The Sea Lion."

Gannon looked at her with a hint of contemplation in his eyes. "You're serious."

"I'm serious. Just think what would happen if we captured evidence of the actual fish. A new, mutated species." She grabbed the magazine. "You could one up this article."

Gannon stared at the article as he popped the blue lollipop back in his mouth.

Sea Lion

Itching to hunt the sea creature before she changed her mind, Bailey had begged Gannon to take her to the Sea Lion as soon as she was released from the hospital. She crept behind him, her sneakers squeaking on the shiny floors. He stopped and she rammed into him, her face squishing against his t-shirt. He smelled like fresh soap.

"Can't you walk more…*quietly*?" he hissed as he craned his neck to look back at her.

"I can't help it. It's my sneakers," she whispered.

"Pick up your feet more," he growled back, narrowing his eyes.

"Fine," she spat back.

He turned away from her, inching slowly through the dark hallway.

"You said no one's here this late," she whispered.

"Not usually, but we still need to be quiet. So, be quiet," he said, wheezing.

She pursed her lips and crept along behind him, close to his heels.

They reached the end of the hallway, and he stopped. Bailey halted with a double squeak of her shoes, warranting a glare from Gannon. She rolled her eyes.

He swiped his badge along a control panel beside the door and the light turned green. The lock on the door clicked, and he pushed it open. They walked through. From where they were perched at the top of a stairway, a dark basement appeared below. The same one he'd taken her to the day he showed her the gaping holes in the metal body of the Sea Lion. She hoped they'd been fixed.

He flicked on a light switch. Fluorescent tubes buzzed to life. He walked down the stairs, and she followed closely as they approached the shiny Sea Lion.

They walked to the front of the underwater vehicle. An extra layer of metal had been crudely welded over the three spots where the holes had been.

"All fixed?" she asked, her voice now a normal volume.

"Supposedly. They took it out for a brief test run."

"Oh." Her heart palpitated. Would they be safe in the bowels of the dark ocean?

"You still want to do this?" His eyes pleaded for a change of heart. "I mean, do you really think we can stop it?"

She could still feel her flask, clutched in her hand, slicing into sea creature flesh. "Yeah… No… I don't know." She shook her head. "I cut it. I know I did. It's not invincible. We have to at least get proof." She found his eyes with hers. "Don't you want evidence of the mutated sea creature?"

His lips thinned and he moved his glasses up the bridge of his nose. "Okay. Let's suit up."

"Suit up?"

"Yeah. We always wear full diving gear. In case anything happens."

She stared at him; her shoulders tightened. When was the last time she'd been on a dive?

"Don't worry. It's just a precaution." He walked along the side of the Sea Lion.

She followed him to the back of the room. Tall shelves lined the concrete walls—stacks of neatly folded wetsuits and oxygen tanks on them. He grabbed a suit, handed it to her, then grabbed another for himself.

Gannon set his shoulder bag on the floor. She nestled hers next to it, then they pulled the suits on. When Gannon had his back to her, she snuck a silver flask from her shoulder bag and slipped it into a pocket in the suit. He grabbed his bag and pulled out a hefty camera.

As he secured the solid strap clamped to each side of the camera around his neck, he looked at her. "Calypso PHOT. It's an amphibious 35mm underwater camera. You want to stop this thing. I want proof."

An unsettling wave of nausea roiled through her stomach. What was she getting him into? Could she really stop a sea monster?

Braydon's blond hair flitted through her thoughts, followed by the terror on the young boy's face as he bobbed on the far side of the wake at Pacific Beach.

Gannon turned back to the shelves and inspected the oxygen tanks. She scoured the room. Something caught her eye—a long, metal rod housing what appeared to be a harpoon, hung on the far wall. It was the most menacing-looking piece of equipment in the room.

"Hey." She tapped Gannon on the back then pointed to the harpoon. "What's that?"

He glanced at the weapon. "Speargun."

"How does it work?"

He frowned. "Foolproof. Pull back the lever until it clicks. Point. Shoot."

"Have you ever used it?"

His eyebrows furrowed. "Once. We had an encounter on a dive with a rather large and venomous lionfish. Things got a little hairy."

"We should take it."

He clenched his jaw.

"Don't worry. It's just a precaution," she said, repeating his words from moments before, trying to smile. Was she convincing him, or herself?

Gannon stared at the weapon, then at her. He inspected the camera dangling from his neck. "Fine. Go grab it."

Bailey sprinted over to the far wall and picked up the speargun. It had real weight to it. She ran her hand along the metal rod, then rested her finger over a lever. "Is this the lever to engage it?"

"Yes. Be careful," he scolded.

Speargun in hand, she walked back over to Gannon.

He picked up a pair of tanks, handing them to her. "We should be prepared for a double tank dive, as a precaution."

She took them, dangling the speargun in one hand and the tanks in the other.

"You look like a much younger, much prettier version of Quint."

"Quint?"

"The sea captain from *Jaws*."

"We're not in a horror film." She shook her head.

"It feels like it." He picked up another pair of tanks then led her back to the Sea Lion, stopping at a ladder running down its side. Tanks in one hand, ladder rungs in the other, he mounted and climbed up.

Bailey set the speargun down carefully, then followed Gannon up the ladder, hauling the tanks.

Standing on the top of the Sea Lion, he opened a circular hatch, stepped down into it, then peeked out. "Hand me the tanks. One set at time."

She did as instructed.

Something inside of her told her that this was the right path. She could feel it. Her lingering doubt dissolved as she handed him the tanks one set at a time. She climbed back down the ladder, retrieved the speargun, then gingerly climbed back up, aware she was holding a lethal weapon.

Gannon was waiting, looking up from the insides of the Sea Lion. She handed him the speargun, then climbed into the core of the metal capsule that would catapult them into the recesses of the dark ocean.

Gannon settled the loaded weapon next to the tanks at the back of the tube. A neon orange, several foot-long capsule sat next to it.

"Transoceanic life raft. Built for survival. Holds food, water, and first aid supplies. It's small, strong, and it inflates in two seconds flat." He pointed at a tube sticking into the side of the capsule. "Gas inflation system. Pulling the lanyard releases the gas in the canister inside. You don't want to be in the way when this thing is released. I've only done it once. Thing shot off like a rocket through the water."

He walked to the front and sat in a chair. A small, round pane of glass provided a tiny view outside. He scanned the controls, flipping switches on and off, checking boxes on a paper secured to a clipboard hanging from a hook. "This will take a few minutes. Stealing the Sea Lion on a crazy mission or not, we need to do the minimum check before we roll her out to the pier." He continued switching and checking.

"Fine with me." The minimum checks, wetsuits, and oxygen tanks were precautionary only. At least, that's what she told herself. Despite her instincts that this whole thing was a crazy idea and that she might regret pressuring Gannon into it, she knew it was the only way to redeem Braydon's demise and make the ocean safe again.

Time passed, the minutes ticking by in a painful crawl. Bailey fidgeted in her seat. She wanted to get this show on the road.

Finally, Gannon ticked the last box. "We're ready." He regarded her. "Or, as ready as we'll be. Shall we proceed to steal the Sea Lion?"

"Stop it. You're not stealing. You're authorized to man the Sea Lion."

"On scheduled operations. Never alone."

"You're not alone. You have me."

"You're unauthorized. That I even let you in here is grounds enough for my expulsion."

"Expulsion?" She snorted. "Are you in grade school?"

"Shut up." He turned his head, concealing a smirk. "Taking you out *in* the Sea Lion… Well, that's enough for my career to go up in flames."

"We'll get proof of your mutated species. Then it won't matter that we took the Sea Lion. I promise." She placed her hand on his arm.

He rolled his eyes. "Why do I let you manipulate me?"

"'Cause you like me. And 'cause you want to put a stop to all this too. Even though you don't swim in the water, you love the ocean as much as I do."

He nodded and shrugged.

"And 'cause you don't want harm to come to your beloved sea creatures. Who knows. Maybe you'll get credit in your geeky sea science magazine for identifying a new species."

His eyebrows raised.

"It could happen."

"Whatever. Right now, let's focus on letting the Sea Lion stretch her legs." He pushed a button, and the Sea Lion roared to life.

Gannon pushed another button and a garage door lifted before them. The shoreline opened up, the vast, dark ocean world ahead. As he released a lever, the Sea Lion rolled on her land wheels through the open door, over the rough, sandy beach, seeking the dark depths of the unknown.

Into the Deep

The Sea Lion coasted easily over the surface of the open water. Bailey peered through the small, circular window carved into its metal nose, scouring the only view of the dark water.

She stole a glance at Gannon.

He stared straight ahead, hands hovering over the controls.

"You okay over there, Captain Gannon?" She smirked.

He smiled, shaking his head. "Yeah. Fine. Just questioning my sanity. I don't know how I let you talk me into this. I really don't."

"I told you. You want a picture of a new species, discovered by Doctor Gannon Harley."

His face flushed. He didn't respond.

"Just think. You'll be the famous sea creature doctor." She giggled.

"Are you scared?" he asked.

She swallowed, looking ahead through the small window as they blasted past the wake. "Nah." She could hear the doubt in her voice.

"C'mon. It's *me.*" He sighed. "I'll be honest… I'm shitting my pants over here. I'm not like you."

"Not like *me?* The lifeguard scared of the water." She snorted.

"You know what I mean. You take life by the balls. You go out there, take risks, do what you want. I live in an office closed in by four safe walls, looking at the ocean from my window."

"Gannon, the other day, when I went past the wake…that was the first time I surfed in…five years."

"I didn't realize it had been that long. I know it was because of Braydon."

"Yeah."

"But you surf over at the Wave House all the time."

She shook her head. "Yeah. I ride fake waves closed in by a plastic wall and a fake beach. Real brave." She bit back a surge of tears. What was wrong with her? All this emotion sickened her. Right now, she could really go for a night of mind-numbing shots and rocker sex. No feelings. Just pleasure. Living in the moment.

"There are lots of people who are too scared to even get on a board at the Wave House. Those waves are ferocious. Just like the real thing. Then, you go out there, alone, knowing there is something out there. Maybe even the same thing that killed Braydon, while you watched. And it bit you for Christ's sake."

"What's your point?" She glared at him.

"Give yourself a little credit and admit you're not a scaredy cat." He laughed. The Sea Lion burst past the wake. "Are you scared now? I mean, this *is* crazy."

Dark clouds concealed the usual array of sparkling stars, casting a gloomy hue over the midnight sky. She knew that she had every reason to be scared, but turning back wasn't an option. Not now.

She took a deep breath, shrugged her shoulders, then exhaled long and slow. "Yeah, I'm scared."

"Well, that makes two of us then. And hey, we're in this together."

"We are." She unzipped the pocket in the chest of her wetsuit and pulled out a silver flask, a simple replacement for the one she'd lost after slicing the fish. She unscrewed the top and tilted it against her lips. The alcohol eased her nerves the second it hit her tongue. As it burned down her throat, her body relaxed.

"Resourceful," Gannon said.

"You want some?" She handed him the flask.

"Ummm…" His mouth contorted into a weird line.

"C'mon. This isn't the time to be a square. It'll take the edge off. One sip."

"Why do I listen to you?" He grabbed the flask and took a drink. He choked on the burn, then recovered with a gulp, handing the flask back to her.

She capped it, tightened the seal, then slid it back into the pocket, pulling the zipper up over it.

A loud beep resounded through the small capsule.

Gannon jerked his head down to a dial. "Sonar reading is unusual. We haven't even gone below the surface yet."

"You think it's our fish?"

"Dunno."

A purple hue shimmered ahead, just beneath the surface.

Bailey lurched forward. The water turned green again. "You see that?"

"Yeah. Gotta be our monster. It wouldn't pick up on our heat. We're insulated by the Sea Lion."

"The purple light… It was just there. Now it's gone."

"The fish probably went under."

"We need to follow it," she cried. "Don't let it get away."

"Just wait. See if it comes up again. Watch for the light. The sonar reading has died down." He pointed at the dial. The needle had gone down close to zero again.

"It's going to get away," she shrieked.

"No, it won't. We just detected it. It can't be that far. If we submerge without any idea of what direction it's going, we could lose it entirely. Trust me." His eyes became intense, serious.

She slumped back in the chair. This time she wasn't going home without a fish corpse. No way.

The Sea Lion glided at high speed. The radiance from the moon shimmered off the surface. Gray clouds drifted over them, dimming the light. The surface grew darker still.

A loud blip pierced the silence.

Bailey startled, staring out the window.

Gannon checked the dial. "We have something."

A purple iridescent sheen stretched over the surface ahead, reaching around the Sea Lion. The light undulated. Rays of moonlight amplified the black-purple ripples in the water.

The sonar pinged, louder each time.

Gannon declared, "It's getting closer."

Bailey stared out the window. "Don't ease up."

"I won't."

The purple vanished in a flash. The beeps continued at the same steady rate.

Bailey gasped. "Where is it?"

"It must be underneath us. It can't be far, or we wouldn't be detecting any sonar."

"We need to go down after it," Bailey asserted.

Gannon frowned as he shook his head.

"We can't lose it."

"Okay. Okay." He eased the controls and the Sea Lion slowed then lowered beneath the surface of the water.

The brilliance of the moon vanished. Twinkles from any stars peeking through the clouds were gone. The purple hue was nowhere to be found. Darkness cloaked them. The steady blip, blip of the sonar rang through their ears.

Where are you, fucking fish? Bailey stared straight out of the window into the black, underwater world. She wanted to find the purple glowing light. To see the pulsing, light bulb eyeball dangling from the end of a slimy tentacle-arm, plunging back into a scaly head. To confront the bulbous body of the monster she was hunting.

Gannon had gone silent. The water turned a gloomy shade of navy as they descended. The steady blip-blip gained speed and volume.

Gannon broke his silence. "We're at one hundred meters."

"You think it's below us?"

"Must be. If it was ahead or above, we'd see the purple glow. And the sonar keeps getting stronger."

Bailey's muscles tensed. How long had it been since she'd been this far down? "How deep can this thing go?"

"Don't worry. The Sea Lion can handle forty-five hundred meters below. Seafloor exploration with a DVS started back in the early sixties. The Alvin. It's us humans that are the problem. We can only handle a few hundred meters with diving equipment."

Her breathing quickened into short, sharp breaths that stung the back of her throat.

"Nearly one hundred and fifty now." He fixated on the pocket in her wetsuit. "Take another swig of that battery acid."

"Aren't you funny." She shrugged, then complied. The burn was better than last time and the buzz was stronger. Not enough to stifle the suffocating sensation encompassing her or to ease the pace of her heartbeat. She offered the flask to Gannon.

"I'm fine." He stayed focused on the descent and the blipping sonar.

She screwed the cap on and slid the flask back into her pocket. "All right then. Let's get this fish."

The blipping was like a panicked heartbeat. Her own heart matched its rhythm. Perspiration moistened her face. She licked her lips.

Gannon stayed quiet. She followed suit. What she wouldn't give for a cherry lollipop. Why hadn't she brought any? *Because that's stupid. You're hunting a sea monster.*

A flash of purple blazed through the small window, igniting the water surrounding them and blinding her. The light vanished leaving her vision blurred with dots of color.

"You see anything?" she yelled.

"Just bright light," he yelled back.

Another flash of purple light morphed the world around her into a dazzling blur.

The blipping sonar peaked. The beeps were out of control.

"Goddamn it," Bailey yelled as she blinked rapidly.

"I can't see a damn thing." Gannon cried, his voice higher than she'd ever heard it.

The view through the window cleared. A massive shadow floated over the remnants of the flash of light.

Her heart thumped hard against her chest and thrummed through her ears as Bailey forced herself to focus on the shadow, willing the beast that cast it to show itself. It was now or never.

She stole a glance at Gannon. His hands trembled over the controls.

What had she done? She was down here because of her obsession with Braydon's death. That was fine. But Gannon… He was down here because of her. She couldn't be responsible for his demise.

The shadow loomed, growing, moving over the small window, casting a cloak over the Sea Lion, into its core, turning their metal capsule into an oppressive space.

The sonar blips squealed at an all-time high decibel.

Gannon flung the strap of his underwater camera around his neck and positioned the frame. The purple light glowed, the shadow moved through it, toward them. At them.

Stinky Fish

There it was, right in from of them, obscuring their view into the ominous underwater world.

It hovered, facing them head-on, as if it was ready to hunt. The sea creature scintillated, sending bursts of purple light through the aqua ocean.

Veins slithered over the glowing bulb, its dead center a crimson spot, like a blood pupil.

The slimy tentacle stretched its claw over the bulb, the thick rope-like arm attaching back into the head of the fish.

But this wasn't just a fish. This was a mutated monster of the sea.

A razor-sharp trio of glassy shards glinted in the water with sharpened sea talon tips.

It propelled forward, coming for them.

Bailey gasped. "Holy shit."

The darkness glowed—purple, blue, orange, red—turning the ocean around them into a sonic pulsing light show. Like a death metal rage in the dark depths of a dive basement bar. As the light emitted from the bulb, Bailey couldn't pull herself from it. Her mind blurred and images from a night at *Thrusters,* the heaviest of the metal joints in San Diego, materialized as if she was there now. As she relived the most intense show she'd ever experienced, the ocean and the fish dissolved from her senses. The devil's music blasted through her eardrums and body odor assaulted her nostrils.

"Bailey!" Gannon's voice jarred her back.

"What?" The cracked window and the huge fish materialized.

"You were in a trance or something. Don't stare too long at the bulb."

"Okay. What do we do?"

Gannon grabbed the camera hanging around his neck and moved to the window. "Get proof."

He positioned the camera and pushed a button. A flash of light illuminated the dark ocean. The fish shuddered, then launched, gaining speed.

"The flash. It irritated the fish." Bailey told herself not to back down.

Gannon clicked the camera several more times, causing bright flickers of light.

The fish continued to gain speed. Gannon's hands shook as he backed away from the window. "I've really pissed it off."

"You said the Sea Lion is made of steel, didn't you?"

"Not grade A steel. This isn't the Alvin. I told you."

"Well, it's still steel. We'll be fine."

Gannon stared at her, his face pale and moist. He nodded, then rammed his hand against the controls. The Sea Lion made a slow retreat from the glowing bulbous sea creature.

She watched his Adam's apple bob as he swallowed. "Don't barf."

"I might."

She stared ahead. Gannon pushed down full throttle, and the Sea Lion surged. The creature was gaining on them far too fast. The purple bulb turned scarlet. The water surrounding them morphed into a blood ocean.

Bailey snuck a glance at Gannon. She didn't want his blood joining the toxic ocean cocktail. She needed to make sure he made it. Even if she didn't. The blood eye-bulb flickered. The fish came into full view. The tentacle wove through the water, searching its way, providing a guide for the monster. The mouth opened and closed in rhythm to the pulsing, bloody light, revealing glassy fangs in search of food. Seeking flesh.

Waves of water washed over the Sea Lion, rippling around the body of the metal cylinder.

Scarlet light beamed as the creature's mouth stretched wider. Glassy fangs glimmered as the monster loomed over the window.

"Holy crap!" Gannon howled.

Bailey's instincts clawed at her gut. She stared into the entrancing radiance.

Sea monster met Sea Lion in a crash of epic proportions. A massive bang rang through the marine explorer, quaking their bodies in seismic tremors.

Darkness descended, knocking Bailey out for a split second. Her eyes popped open. She stared at the oculus, watching it dim to a soft, blue hue. Black blood poured from the creature's mouth through the aqua depths. It backed away, revealing a sliver of steel protruding from the front of the DVS lodged in the top of its mouth. The shard released from the fish flesh, exposing a slash across the gums of the monster, above its middle fang.

Fissures crackled across the circular window and water trickled in. The reading on the control panel indicated they were two hundred meters down. Gannon had said they could only survive a few hundred, with gear. What did he mean by *a few?*

"Fuck." Bailey exhaled.

Gannon shook his head, seeming disoriented. A red gash split his forehead. Cracks wove through the left lens of his glasses.

Damn it. She couldn't let him die.

She watched the fish as it retreated.

It's hurt.

She analyzed Gannon's state. Blood trickled over his glasses. "You okay?"

He shook his head, his curls tainted with thick scarlet. "Yeah. I'm fine." He stared out the cracked window. "The Sea Lion is compromised."

"A little water."

"It's okay. Look. The fish…it's backing away. Perhaps the Lion did some damage."

"I'm sure it did."

The fish stopped. The light blue hue of the bulb blazed purple, then crimson again.

Gannon exclaimed, "Oh no. Looks like it's recovering."

"You're right."

The fish lurched. It rushed them, as black liquid oozed from its gums, mixing with the water.

Gannon wailed. "We can't turn around fast enough. We need to ram it. Head-on."

"You sure?" Her gut seized. She knew he was right. They'd come this far. But she didn't like the look of Gannon. The gash across his forehead. His pale face.

"Never been more sure about anything." Gannon braced himself.

She swallowed back the doubt. "Okay." She concentrated on the fish.

Gannon rammed on the throttle again.

The Sea Lion plunged through the stained ocean. The metal cylinder rumbled as it rammed into the massive monster.

Gannon's head smashed against the window. Blood poured over his face.

Glassy fangs pierced steel.

Fresh holes plunged straight through the front end of the Sea Lion. Bursts of water streamed in several spouts, creating mini waterfalls. Fissures rippled. Glass cracked. Murky water poured through the window into the capsule.

The fish retreated, pulling glassy fangs from metal, smearing the ocean in black.

Gannon shook his head, trying to focus through cracked glasses. He raised his hand, clutched his spectacles, and rubbed his head with his other hand. "We need to get out." His voice sounded far away.

The stitch in Bailey's gut intensified. Water poured in all around them. They were going down. She needed to get Gannon out of here. She racked her brain, contemplating the best course of action as water burst through the cracked window in streams.

The fish backed away, its internal fluids snaking through the water.

It was wounded, but still alive. Her mission wouldn't be complete until it was dead.

Gannon moaned.

She pulled herself from the seat, scanning the bowels of the DVS. Her eye caught a stack of flares and the capsule-shaped life raft. She sprung through the body of the Sea Lion, grabbing the items. As she threw them down beside Gannon, he moaned louder.

"Gannon, stay with me. You're gonna be fine."

She grabbed the neon life raft and unraveled the rope around it. Winding the rope around Gannon, she tied the ends in a tight knot.

"Gannon, can you stand up?"

He nodded groggily, then attempted to stand. His knees buckled and he crumpled to the ground, hunched over and wheezing.

Think Bailey. A frantic search landed her gaze on the oxygen tanks. She grabbed a set, maneuvered the mouthpiece into Gannon's mouth, then engaged the airflow. He took several breaths, the color returning to his face. He stood and worked with her to secure the tanks onto his back then waited as she hoisted a single tank over her own back. She flung his arm over her neck, wrapped an arm around his waist, grabbed the life raft, and guided him across the hull.

"You have to get up the ladder," she said.

He nodded then started to climb, unsteadily. Using her own body weight, she forced him up.

She unlatched the first cylindrical hatch, pushing him through it, headfirst, followed by the life raft. Scrambling up behind him, she secured the first hatch. Repeating her steps, she guided him through the second hatch, into the ocean.

Cranking the airflow of her own tank, she took a deep breath from her mouthpiece, then stuck her head through.

Gannon drifted above the Sea Lion, his eyes closing as he started to slip into unconsciousness. His copper curls floated through the dark aqua world.

She pulled the lanyard attached to the gas inflation system with a swift pop. Air filled the raft with a whoosh. The raft shot through the water, taking Gannon with it.

Gannon's body looked like a rag doll, the raft shooting up past him, dragging him along as it made a massive sprint for the surface of the dark ocean.

Bile stung her throat. The instinctual claw released its grasp on her gut. She knew she'd done the right thing.

Bailey grabbed a flare and aimed it at Gannon's body, now only a small dot shooting for the surface. The trigger clicked as she pulled it. A whoosh sounded and a bright flare blazed through the water, as light illuminated the darkness. She hoped it reached the surface.

Grabbing another flare, she shot it off the same way. Then another. Several fire comets sailed through the depths to the surface.

Willing herself to trust that Gannon would make it and the life raft would inflate, she descended back into the Sea Lion, securing both doors behind her.

Hunt

Rumbling erupted from the front of the Sea Lion. Fissures continued to crawl through the window, splitting in all directions. The ocean gushed in, stronger by the second. Metal bolts vibrated, loosening from their nuts. One of them shot out across the hull. A cascade of water followed, flooding the floor.

Bailey surveyed her quickly deteriorating underwater home. Finding the one remaining tank propped up at the back, she waded through the thigh-high water, not wanting to face the depths on a single tank.

An aggressive burst submerged the tank. She took a breath from her mouthpiece, submerged, and searched the floor. There it was, lodged in the corner. She grabbed the tank and resurfaced. Now chest-deep in the rising flood, she attached the second tank to her back and checked the pressure. The needle swung into position. She breathed in, then out. The oxygen in the tank responded.

Her eyes darted around the DVS. She lunged for the speargun and grabbed it with both hands. *I'm coming for you, fucking fish.*

Water circled her shoulders as she steadied herself and sought the front of the Sea Lion. The bolts securing the metal frame, holding the cracking window in place, flew out one by one like metal darts.

Water poured in and the window gave way.

Shards of glass flew in all directions. Bailey ducked into the water, covering her head with her arms, losing the speargun. A piece of glass shot past her, slicing the arm of her wetsuit.

Streams followed, filling the insides of the Sea Lion. The water ate Bailey up. A jolt of panic shot through her.

No.

She surfaced, took a deep breath, then retrieved the speargun as it drifted by. It engaged with a loud click as she yanked on the lever. Lunging forward, she reached her arms out in front of her, clutching the speargun in one hand, then swam toward the nose of the Sea Lion.

Reaching the gaping hole where the window once was, she moved her arms in powerful strokes, kicking her legs. Her body thrust into the depths of the ocean.

No light. No purple sonic eyeball. Only aqua darkness.

Shadows fluttered around her. Bursts of bubbles filtered through the black water. Engulfed in the deep underwater world, she couldn't spot her prey. Her gut told her that it was close by.

Bailey swam into the dark nothing, searching for a sea monster.

Die

The dark water vortex swirled, pulling Bailey down into the black, unknown depths. Acid-laced bile clawed up her throat. She swallowed against it, told it to go fuck itself, and braced herself to face the underwater world.

Holy fuck. What am I doing?

The motion of the water pulled her down. Palpitations hijacked her heart, sending tremors through her entire body.

Focus.

She took a slow breath, easing up on her depletion of the oxygen tank.

Breathe.

She tilted her head down, stared into the darkness, and let go of all control.

Think of Braydon.

Her fish was down there, somewhere in the ominous underwater world. She knew it.

An iridescent, purple glow pulsed beneath her, casting a hue through the black water. Every neuron in her brain vibrated.

The spinning slowed and the water vortex dissolved. Nothingness caved in on her, creating a sense of suffocation. Her heart skipped a couple of beats. Her body froze and drifted, weightless.

Strange vibrations of sound echoed through the space around her. It was the sound of creatures living deep below the natural living space of the human species. Heart rate slowing, oxygen depletion easing up, she turned her head back and forth, strands of hair floating around her like sea snakes of a marine Medusa.

The purple hue glowed through the water like rays from an outer space sun. No movement. No sound. A bulbous shadow cast through the watery depths ahead.

Baily swallowed, gripping the speargun and aiming it at the silhouette.

The outline grew as it crawled through the water.

What the fuck? Fighting against the resistance of the deep, she positioned the speargun, following the shadow.

It loomed; its size increased steadily.

Drifting like a mid-afternoon snack, Bailey fixated on the approach of the massive underwater beast, waiting for it to reveal itself.

The shadow shimmered. Deep blue flesh materialized, stretching across a sinister cavern. The hole closed and opened in a rhythm, sucking in everything surrounding it.

Some sea creature. Not her fish.

A school of sardines, eyes protruding from their slimy silver heads, streaked by in a blur. Dozens of eyes stared her down. She shivered. The eyes peered at her as they were sucked into the dark cavern. The mouth closed. The eyes vanished. In a single chomp, dozens of fish were swallowed whole. Some were chomped in half. Distended eyeballs peered from floating heads. Jagged jaw marks cut grotesque patterns into the severed necks and scarlet swirls seeped from exposed interiors.

The heads drifted by, their mouths still gaping open in a death breath. The stitch in her gut returned with might. The cavern-mouthed fish swam away. A rush of water whirled over her as the fin swept back and forth, leaving her in a gloomy current.

Her blood stilled in her veins and her eyes refused to blink.

Vibrations caused ripples of movement around her. She slow-motion jerked left, then right, searching for the source. Strange sounds shook her body, drumming her skull. Was it her fish? Or other creatures stirring? Suddenly, the ocean turned still and silent.

She floated and waited.

A bright flash of light electrified the water around her. She blinked hard, staring into the iridescence—purple, blue, aqua—mixed in a cosmic ray. Bailey stared into it, clutching the speargun with both of her trembling hands, waiting.

It appeared out of nowhere. A bright bulb, purple veins snaking over it, a blood-red pupil. It entranced her, pulling her gaze into its core. The dark ocean depths swirled around her in a haze.

No, she screamed through her own mind, snapping herself from the strange trance the light was pulling her into.

It doesn't win.

The eyeball stared. She held the speargun tight in one hand, swam through the water with the other, kicking her legs behind. The purple light pulsed brighter. She squinted into the psychedelic blaze.

Then she saw it, the fish in its entirety.

The fish lunged, opening its mouth to reveal three fangs sharpened to lethal points. The eyeball probed through the water on a long tentacle with scaly fingers cradling the bulb. Its body glowed in a fluorescent purple, iridescent blue, shimmering aqua underwater light show. Its fangs reached for her, instinctively knowing where to find fresh flesh.

With a sudden jolt, the fish blazed through the ocean depths straight for her.

No. You don't win. Braydon wins.

Bailey raised her arms, pointing the end of the speargun at the hypnotic bulb. She kicked her legs hard, slicing through the water, gunning for her marine prey.

A sudden current from the movement of the creature dragged Bailey sideways. The speargun dislodged from her grip. Fangs sliced through the water. A buzz of panic hijacked her brain. The purple hue turned red. The fangs scissored through the water, slashing their way to their feast.

Kill it. She screamed to herself.

The needle on one of her oxygen tanks rocked a notch down. *Fuck.*

The spear glinted, out of the corner of her eye.

The fish attacked. The fangs closed a half inch from her, one of them severing her wetsuit across her chest.

Bailey snapped herself to attention, kicked her legs and shot her arms out in front of her, pushing the water at the fish, propelling herself away. She searched the spot where she'd seen the speargun. It was lodged in the crack of a porous rock. Using her arm and leg as propellors, she pushed another wave into the fangs, shooting herself closer to the gun.

She squinted into the swirling underwater wave she'd formed, finding the fluorescent, fanged fish. The veiny eyeball rolled back and forth, confused by the onslaught of underworld current. She swam for the speargun. Yanking it with all her might, she dislodged it from the rocky crevice then searched the water, seeking the hunter that now was her prey.

The water settled. The red hue deepened, sending a blood light through the underwater world. The fangs pierced the water, seeking her in lethal chomps.

Fuck it.

Bailey aimed the speargun directly at the blood-red pupil.

The eyeball wove through the water, its veins slithering over the white bulb, seeking flesh. Seeking her.

Focus.

The fangs closed in on her.

Breathe.

A foul stench burst through the bloody depths, seeping into her face mask, pumping through the tube into her mouth. She gagged. The smell of a rotting carcass infested with maggots seeped into her mouth, her eyes, her nose.

Acid swam up her throat. She swallowed against it.

This ends now.

Bailey pulled the breathing tube from her mouth and screamed, sending a chilling cry up her throat, out her mouth, and through the water. The eyeball halted. The fangs stilled. Bailey shoved the breather back into her mouth and took a long pull of oxygen. The needle jumped lower, almost empty.

For Braydon.

Kicking her legs as hard as she could, she sent every ounce of energy through her clenching muscles. She thrusted at the sea creature. The fangs opened then clamped down, sliding into her wetsuit, piercing three bloody caverns into her arm.

Pain seared the holes in her flesh, like three hot coals, branding her from the inside.

She pointed the end of the speargun against the red pupil and pulled the trigger.

A burst of black-purple sea creature blood exploded from the bulb, flooding the water. Gills seized. Bubbles ruptured from the slits, shooting a fresh wave of rotting stench through the water.

An ungodly sound shook through the ocean. Her hands shot over her ears as the speargun drifted downwards.

The monster turned onto its side. The black-purple blood clouded the water. Tattered remnants of the eye retreated, the tentacle pulling it back into its scaly body.

Bailey's entire body seized. Her own scarlet cloud plumed through the water from her wounds. She halted all function as she slowed her breathing and quieted the buzzing in her brain.

The needle on the second oxygen tank plunged close to zero.

Fish blood shot from the creature's still gills. Dim flickers of purple light fought against the murkiness as the sea creature sank down into the depths.

Bailey slipped the tanks off her back. She thrust her arms straight up over her head, forming a straight line, then pushed down against the resistance of the water. Kicking her legs with all her might, her body shot upwards.

Snatching a flare clasped to her belt, she fired it. It was an underwater comet seeking the surface. Her last hope.

Easing into a rhythm, she repeated the motions with her arms and legs, fighting against the heavy water. Her body rocketed through the ocean in time with her propulsions.

Echoes of the dying fish still rang in her ears as the remnants of purple light electrified her eyes. Scarlet streams from the holes in her arm and leg snaked through the water. Who knew what other creatures it would attract?

She stroked and kicked. The water lightened from black to dark blue.

Her brain buzzed on the brink of unconsciousness.

Drowsiness made her mind whirl and her eyelids heavy as she stroked and kicked, the life draining from her. The navy blue surrounding her softened to aqua. Rays of sunlight shone through the water ceiling above. She looked up at the light, fighting off the dizziness. Her mind turned blank as her body went limp and she floated.

Surface

Bailey tried to blink, but she could swear her eyes were glued shut.

Where am I?

She pried her eyes open, cringing against the ripping sensation. The world came to life around her in a haze—a swirl of yellow and orange.

She blinked hard, several times, her eyelids sticky against her eyeballs. Her eyelashes rough with salt and scales.

What the fuck happened?

A purple light flashed. Pointy fangs lunged at her. Tremors rang through her ears. She shook her head and sat up. Hot needles stuck into her arm. Three holes pierced through her wetsuit into her flesh, hot blood pouring from them.

"Bailey," a faraway voice called. "Bailey!"

She twisted her neck, holding her head, scanning around her, and saw a face. A familiar face.

Copper tousled curls. Crooked spectacles. A cracked lens.

"Gannon!" Her throat cracked. She swallowed. Not a drop of moisture was available.

"Are you *okay?*" Concern washed over him. He had a deep gash across his forehead.

The sea creature had rammed the Sea Lion, causing Gannon's head to hit the window.

It all came rushing back to her in a flood of horrific images. She had put his life on the line. But he was okay. She was okay.

How was she here?

She looked around. They were sitting in the now inflated, bright orange life raft. It was larger than she deemed possible, given the size of the airless capsule. A thin roof sheltered them. The sides of the door flapped open, revealing a blood-orange sunrise.

Gannon peered at her in his battered, bloody state. Tempted to pinch herself, she couldn't believe he'd survived his launch from the depths of the ocean after the hard hit he took to his head.

"Are you okay?" he repeated.

Her salty sour odor stung her nostrils. "Yeah." Her voice sounded a little less far away. "Are you?"

Gannon's eyes widened. She would swear he was excited. "I'm great. You saved me."

"I guess I did." She touched the unzipped pocket of her wetsuit where the flask had been. The pocket was empty. Oh yeah. She had drained it and dropped it on the Sea Lion floor.

"What happened down there?" he asked, eyes wide.

She smirked. "I got it. With a speargun to the eyeball."

"Holy shit." Gannon giggled. "I can't believe you shot me up here with this life raft." His voice rang through her throbbing brain. "You're like a female MacGyver."

She smiled. "Whatever."

"The sudden movement and cold water shook me awake. I came to, and I was drifting beside the raft. Still tied to it. I told you, these things are designed to rocket to the surface then inflate." He frowned. "I didn't see you anywhere. Then…all of the sudden you were floating a few feet away. I paddled over with my hands and pulled you into the raft. You gave me a real scare." He threw his hands into the air. "You'll never guess what happened."

"Besides the destruction of your precious Sea Lion and the attack of the killer fish?"

"That doesn't matter."

"What?" She sat up straighter, leaning back against the life raft.

Gannon lifted his underwater camera. "My camera. It's intact. The photos, they'll be fine."

Her mind cleared. "What?"

"My photos. Before that fucker rammed the Sea Lion, I got a couple of good ones. Actual proof of a mutated sea creature. A new species."

"I'll be damned." She couldn't help but giggle.

"I'll be in *Popular Science* for sure." He looked happy and relaxed. Was that possible? "Proves my theory. Sea Lion won't matter. This is way bigger than a second-class DVS system. Now we'll get our own Alvin."

Bailey sunk back into the cushioned side of the life raft. The sun peeked over the horizon, turning it from blood-orange into a soft tangerine-pink hue.

Bailey stared solemnly at the 666 scratched crudely over the 720, next to the black door, wondering if it was a fresh assault of graffiti or if they'd neglected to repaint the sign the last time it happened. The joint between her fingers dwindled as she took a last drag.

Reclining against the wall and concealing the devil's number, she released the smoke in a long exhale. Out near the end of the pier, a red-orange hue glowed over the horizon past the wake. Little sparkles dotted the ocean like golden gems. She knew why she hadn't left all those years ago when the purple iridescent fanged fish bit into the one person she loved. After she'd watched him bleed out scarlet streams into the deep aqua and she'd stared in frozen fear while his body slipped underneath the surface, while the water pulled him down to his watery grave. She loved it here too much. Top that off with the instinct churning in her belly, telling her she had to stay and that someday she would get all the answers she needed about what had happened that day.

Exhaling the last puff of herbal relaxation, she flicked the butt onto the pavement and stamped it out with her black buckled boot. She scanned herself, running her eyes along her shiny red pleather and black tank top with bold lettering bleeding down the front declaring her to be a fan of Angels of Death. She'd gone all out tonight even if she wasn't sure why. Resisting the temptation to crawl into her bed and hide from the world, she didn't feel ready for this, but she knew she would no longer cower.

Facing the fangs that bit Braydon had stirred up a lot of painful memories. She'd poured herself into her relationship with him. Given him everything she had. The years of numbing the pain with Jack Daniel's and heavy metal had helped her push the horrific pain that had ripped through her into an internal crevice. She hadn't planned on ever digging it out. When she faced the sea monster that took Braydon from her, the crevice ripped open. Fresh pain sliced through her, consuming her as if she was back there on that day.

She stared at the entrance to 720. What was she doing here anyway? *Dammit.* Rhys had flung open another closed door deep within her. The one that secured any remnant of *feeling* she could possibly have for anyone else. Superficial nights of losing herself in rock and booze, arousing her senses with loud music and meaningless sex, had stimulated her. It had kept her occupied, prevented her from actually *feeling* anything more than a temporary buzz that would leave her depleted and unsatisfied.

She sighed as she watched the tangerine sunset. What else would she do?

Fuck it.

The door swung swiftly as she yanked it open and barged into the dimly lit, stuffy joint before she could change her mind. *One drink. One song.* Maybe, if the band was decent, she'd lounge at the back, enjoy a couple of beers, and people-watch. There was no need for her to stay the whole show or stalk the lead singer for a private after-party. *Yeah.* A chill evening, enjoying the music she loved, might help her to rewrite her routine. She half snorted. It wasn't a bad idea.

Her shoulders relaxed when she saw Johnny serving drinks. His energy would lift her up, and he was a good listener.

Bailey hoisted herself up onto one of the high bar chairs. Could she really do it? Test out a new routine? It might mean she wouldn't have to kick her love for metal out of her life.

Johnny slid up to the bar, smiling wide. "How are you, girl? Wasn't sure if you'd be in anytime soon."

"Yeah, well, can't miss a show." She forced a weak smile.

"Did you really go after that monster fish? You crazy bitch."

"I did."

Johnny slapped his palms onto the bar. "You've got bigger balls than me." He paused. "Did you really steal an underwater submarine thingy?"

She smirked. "Well, not really. I mean, my friend, he works at Scripps…"

"Gannon." Johnny nodded. "He came here, when you were in the hospital, looking for some tunes for you."

"The Angels of Death cassette." Rhys' voice was the only thing that had calmed her shattered nerves while she was stuck in the hospital bed. "Well, he has access to this underwater thingy. And it's not a submarine. It's a DVS. The Sea Lion."

"Wow. I don't even know who you are anymore. And not in a bad way. I'm impressed."

"Well, at least one of us is. I'm just tired."

"I bet. Look at you, though. All cut up, bruised, battered, and you still look stunning. I love those red pants." He eyed up and down her legs.

She giggled. "Johnny. Stop it."

"I mean it." He slid back behind the bar. "You look amazing. Ready for another lead singer? Saw them earlier when they were setting up. He's just your type."

She looked down at the bar. "Nah. I'm gonna pass tonight."

"What? You okay?" His eyes pleaded with her.

"Yeah. Really, I am. I'm just…tired. I need to chill."

"Can I get you your usual?"

"I'll take a cream ale."

"No Jack?"

She blushed. "Well, maybe one."

He winked as he set a shot glass on the bar. He filled it, making an extra show of how high he could raise the bottle and still get the liquid into the glass with the utmost precision.

Sweet oak wafted over to Bailey. She took a deep breath. Rhys fluttered through her thoughts as she stared at the drink. Johnny mumbled something as he fished for a beer in the bar fridge. The room blurred around her and her mind wandered. An electric buzz soared through her as she relived Rhys' private show for her. His eyes had explored her in a way that no one else's ever had.

Johnny snapped the can onto the counter with a loud click. "Hey, Bailey. You with me?" Concern riddled his face.

Her cheeks blazed. "Yeah. Sorry." She shook her head. "Like I said. I'm just tired. I'm gonna hang for a bit, check out the band, then head out early."

"Say, this doesn't have anything to do with that show the other night? Angels of Death?" His mouth screwed up in contemplation.

She looked down at her shirt.

His eyes followed hers. He laughed. "Ah. I see. It has everything to do with them and that raven-haired lead singer. You seemed different around him. Not like you usually are when you're on the hunt for a rock dude to eat up and spit out."

"Hey now."

"Well, am I wrong?"

Bailey contemplated how to defend herself. She couldn't think of any logical argument. He'd probably know if she was lying anyway. "No. You're not wrong." She took a long pull of the cream ale.

"So, you go on this big adventure, nearly die, save the beach, and you won't even let yourself celebrate a little?"

She took another pull of the beer, glaring at him. "Don't you have customers to serve?"

Johnny surveyed the bar. "They've all been served. In the midst of the big adventure to kill the sea monster wreaking havoc on the beach, you finally meet a treat that is more than just tasty. You liked him. For real. Now you have all these *feelings* to deal with."

She scowled at him.

He faced her with his arms crossed.

"Fine. You're right. About all of it. But what the hell am I supposed to do? I'm sitting here without any appetite for my usual guilty pleasures, I'm wearing fucking red pants, and all I can think about is an insanely talented singer who smells like vanilla." She threw her hands up in the air, then dropped them back on the bar.

Johnny pouted. "Ah, I'm sorry."

A hoot came from the end of the bar.

"They're getting restless down there. I'll be right back." He walked away.

Bailey sat, staring at the Jack Daniel's, a weight sinking to the bottom of her stomach. What *was* she going to do? She'd wanted this. Answers. Closure. Yet, everything seemed so empty now. She shook her head, then shot back the Jack.

Johnny returned, can of cream ale in hand. "My treat. Stop looking so glum."

"Why?" She pouted.

Johnny looked past her, at the door. "Because." He lowered his eyes, finding hers. "You're not doomed to be alone forever, after all."

Bailey gawked at him quizzically.

A vanilla scent seeped up from behind her. Her stomach spun.

A hand touched her shoulder, a metal skull ring perched on the middle finger. As she turned, onyx tresses welcomed her. She looked up into Rhys' dark eyes. Quivers ran over her body. Was she imagining this?

"Bailey. Hoped I'd find you here."

"Rhys." She shook her head. Her voice was a mere whisper. "What are you doing here?"

"Tour got truncated."

"What? Why?" That couldn't be. They were so good.

"We got picked up for an international tour. Smaller gigs got canceled."

"But you're here."

"Got some time before we take off." He took her hand, looking into her eyes. "Bailey, I had to see you. There are things I need to say to you before we leave."

"Really?"

"Yeah."

She took her hand from his. "But you're just leaving again. I'm not sure I want to hear what you have to say."

He ran his fingers down the side of her face. "You won't know until you hear me out."

Bailey's head spun. Vanilla consumed her. She closed her eyes and breathed him in. The wave she'd finally faced fluttered through her mind. *No more fear.*

She opened her eyes. "That, I can do."

"How about a shot of our good friend?"

"Sure." She looked over her shoulder, finding Johnny. He nodded.

"You here for the show? We could hang around, see if they're any good."

Johnny slid two shot glasses to them then slipped away. The familiar sweet sting crept up her nose.

"Your van nearby?"

"Out front." He nodded at the door.

"You got an acoustic?"

He winked. "Never leave home without it."

"Good." She raised the shot glass. "How about a private show at Chez Bailey?"

"I'll toast to that."

They clicked the tiny glasses, shot back the JD, then walked out the back door.

Popular Science

Waves thundered, sending drifts of fresh sea air through the window. Bailey laid back against the fuzzy pink pillow on her bed. She closed her eyes, drinking in the sounds and smells of the ocean. Her home.

She'd taken it back. It was hers again.

A soft moan came from the other side of the bed. Vanilla floated up and around her. She closed her eyes tighter, reached across the bed, and ran her fingers through soft hair.

Rhys drifted off into another round of sleep.

Bailey opened her eyes, slid her legs over the side of the bed, and walked across the room. She curled into the pillow-clad nook in the corner, perched beside the window overlooking the beach and the open ocean. She relished in the early morning when the sun peeked over the far end of the water. An orange-pink glow cast diamonds over the aqua surface. Seagulls squealed in their silly play. The burst of a surfer on the crest of a wave and a curved blue body following, fin poking high, played abreast its human friend. A few lone joggers ran along the shore, feet splashing against the incoming tide. Seashells dotted the wet sand in shiny shards.

She sighed. A calm washed over her—one she hadn't known since Braydon died.

The people from Woods Hole Oceanographic Institution had come by for a visit, bringing the Alvin with them. They'd made a special trip, Gannon aboard, into the depths of the ocean. They'd found the sea monster's corpse. It turned out the fish she had killed in the dark ocean depths was indeed a new species. A comparison of its teeth to the holes that pierced the flesh of the woman that washed up on Mission Beach and the diver scraping against the sea wall in La Jolla, concluded that she'd killed the monster hunting in her beloved ocean. They'd also found sheets of eggs nestled in algae several hundred feet below the surface.

The search had been going on all week. Many eggs were retrieved for inspection, then for disposal. She wondered how they would know if they'd found them all. *Popular Science* was knocking on Dr. Gannon's door. He would soon appear in a full center spread. Funding for the team at Scripps was pouring in.

Bailey knew she'd killed her nemesis. She knew the fish she'd faced was the same one that had ripped its fangs into Braydon.

She looked longingly at her blue and silver board propped up in the corner, ready for her to catch some waves with Dalton later that afternoon.

Dark locks splayed around pink fuzzy pillows caught her eye. But not before she took in her own dose of a metal angel.

THE END?

Not if you want to dive into more of Crystal Lake Publishing's Tales from the Darkest Depths!

Check out our amazing website and online store or download our latest catalog: https://geni.us/CLPCatalog.

We always have great new projects and content on the website to dive into, as well as a newsletter, behind the scenes options, social media platforms, our own dark fiction shared-world series and our very own webstore. Our webstore even has categories specifically for KU books, non-fiction, anthologies, and of course more novels and novellas.

AUTHOR BIOGRAPHY

Julie Hiner spent endless hours during her childhood lost in the pages of books. The only thing that took precedence over a book was her Walkman. Julie remains a hardcore eighties rocker at heart.

Julie worked as a computer scientist, specializing in network simulation. On a break between contracts, she published an inspirational work of nonfiction, her own story of facing fear and anxiety on a bicycle in the European mountains.

Julie now writes psychological horror/suspense heavily infused with hard rock and metal. She has published an eighties metal murder detective series, a nineties nostalgic serial killer novella, a death metal demon possession novella, and co-curated a horror anthology. Several of Julie's horror short stories have been published in anthologies. You can find her at KillersAndDemons.com serving up toxic cocktails of metal and murder.

Readers…

Thank you for reading *Fear of the Deep*. We hope you enjoyed this novel. If you have a moment, please review *Fear of the Deep* at the store where you bought it.

Help other readers by telling them why you enjoyed this book. No need to write an in-depth discussion. Even a single sentence will be greatly appreciated. Reviews go a long way to helping a book sell, and is great for an author's career. It'll also help us to continue publishing quality books.

Thank you again for taking the time to journey with Crystal Lake's Torrid Waters.

You will find links to all our social media platforms on our Linktree page: https://linktr.ee/CrystalLakePublishing.

MISSION STATEMENT

Since its founding in August 2012, Crystal Lake has quickly become one of the world's leading publishers of Dark Fiction and Horror books. In 2023, Crystal Lake officially transitioned into an entertainment company, joining several other divisions, genres, and imprints, including Torrid Waters, Crystal Lake Comics, Crystal Lake Games, Crystal Lake Kids, and many more.

While we strive to present only the highest quality fiction and entertainment, we also endeavour to support authors along their writing journey. We offer our time and experience in non-fiction projects, as well as author mentoring and services, at competitive prices.

With several Bram Stoker Award wins and many other wins and nominations (including the HWA's Specialty Press Award), Crystal Lake Publishing puts integrity, honor, and respect at the forefront of our publishing operations.

We strive for each book and outreach program we spearhead to not only entertain and touch or comment on issues that affect our readers, but also to strengthen and support the Dark Fiction field and its authors.

Not only do we find and publish authors we believe are destined for greatness, but we strive to work with men and women who endeavour to be decent human beings who care more for others than themselves, while still being hard working, driven, and passionate artists and storytellers.

Crystal Lake Publishing is and will always be a beacon of what passion and dedication, combined with overwhelming teamwork and respect, can accomplish. We endeavour to know each and every one of our readers, while building personal relationships with our authors, reviewers, bloggers, podcasters, bookstores, and libraries.

We will be as trustworthy, forthright, and transparent as any business can be, while also keeping most of the headaches away from our authors, since it's our job to solve the problems so they can stay in a creative mind. Which of course also means paying our authors.

We do not just publish books, we present to you worlds within your world, doors within your mind, from talented authors who sacrifice so much for a moment of your time.

There are some amazing small presses out there, and through collaboration and open forums we will continue to support other presses in the goal of helping authors and showing the world what quality small presses are capable of accomplishing. No one wins when a small press goes down, so we will always be there to support hardworking, legitimate presses and their authors. We don't see Crystal Lake as the best press out there, but we will always strive to be the best, strive to be the most interactive and grateful, and even blessed press around. No matter what happens over time, we will also take our mission very seriously while appreciating where we are and enjoying the journey.

What do we offer our authors that they can't do for themselves through self-publishing?

We are big supporters of self-publishing (especially hybrid publishing), if done with care, patience, and planning. However, not every author has the time or inclination to do market research, advertise, and set up book launch strategies. Although a lot of authors are successful in doing it all, strong small presses will always be there for the authors who just want to do what they do best: write.

What we offer is experience, industry knowledge, contacts and trust built up over years. And due to our strong brand and trusting fanbase, every Crystal Lake Publishing book comes with weight of respect. In time our fans begin to trust our judgment and will try a new author purely based on our support of said author.

With each launch we strive to fine-tune our approach, learn from our mistakes, and increase our reach. We continue to assure our authors that we're here for them and that we'll carry the weight of the launch and dealing with third parties while they focus on their strengths—be it writing, interviews, blogs, signings, etc.

We also offer several mentoring packages to authors that include knowledge and skills they can use in both traditional and self-publishing endeavours.

We look forward to launching many new careers.

This is what we believe in. What we stand for. This will be our legacy.

Welcome to Crystal Lake Publishing—Where Stories Come Alive!

Also from Torrid Waters...

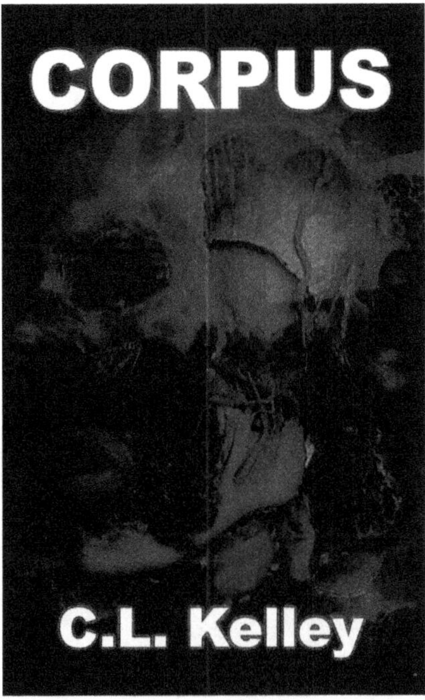

In C.L. Kelley's debut novel Corpus, the city's night transforms into a realm of terror.

Nameless, powerful beings, lost in their hunger and forgotten pasts, roam the streets after sunset. But an awakening stirs within them, sharpening their minds and unearthing memories of a dark history and an even darker future.

This chilling foray into vampire fiction pits the hunter against the hunted in a world brimming with supernatural horror and action. Kelley masterfully intertwines multiple perspectives, each character endowed with unique psychic abilities. At the heart of this narrative is a complex villain protagonist, blurring the lines between hero and villain.

The plot thickens with the presence of shapeshifters, adding layers of unpredictability to the already tense atmosphere. Even the seasoned monster hunters find themselves outmatched by these evolving adversaries. The once comforting break of dawn no longer signifies safety.

C.L. Kelley's Corpus is a thrilling exploration of a world where night creatures are not just real but are becoming something more formidable. It's a tale of survival, where the emergence of the dawn might not end the nightmare.

This novel promises an immersive experience into a spine-tingling universe, where every turn of the page brings you closer to the heart of darkness.

Also from Torrid Waters...

**A fast-paced story of survival,
terror, family, and friendship.**

The people of Wicker thought the mountain belonged to them—purchased with blood, sweat, and resilience. They forgot the deal their ancestors made. They forgot that their mountain belonged to something ancient, powerful, and hungry.

Charlotte Crowe and Rebecca Greenleigh grew up as best friends on the mountain, descendants of the original settlers of Wicker and inheritors of a terrible secret. They expected to grow old on their mountain. They did not expect the return of the wolves, the bone chimes appearing overnight in the trees, or their neighbors turning on one another. In a matter of days, everything they thought they knew is flipped upside down and they find themselves trapped in a place they once called home playing a dangerous game with a creature older than the mountain itself.

THANK YOU FOR PURCHASING THIS BOOK

www.ingramcontent.com/pod-product-compliance
Lightning Source LLC
Chambersburg PA
CBHW070423310726
48977CB00003B/811